T5-CRJ-849

DEC 08 1909

Blairsville High School Library

Blairsville High School Library

Only Birds & Angels Fly

Only Birds & Angels Fly

Blairsville High School Library

FIC
HOR

Joshua Horwitz

Harper & Row, Publishers

The lyrics from "Have You Ever Been to Electric Ladyland?," "Drifting," "Are You Experienced?," and "Castles Made of Sand," all by Jimi Hendrix, are reprinted through the courtesy of Bella Godiva Music, Inc. No other reproductions allowed without authorization from Bella Godiva Music, Inc.

Only Birds and Angels Fly
Copyright © 1985 by Joshua Horwitz
All rights reserved. No part of this book may be used or reproduced in any manner whatsoever without written permission except in the case of brief quotations embodied in critical articles and reviews. Printed in the United States of America. For information address Harper & Row Junior Books, 10 East 53rd Street, New York, N.Y. 10022. Published simultaneously in Canada by Fitzhenry & Whiteside Limited, Toronto.

Library of Congress Cataloging in Publication Data
Horwitz, Joshua.
  Only birds and angels fly.

  Summary: During the turbulent sixties, Danny and charismatic Chris renew the friendship begun in junior high school only to find that sometimes friendship isn't enough to counteract different attitudes toward life.
  [1. Friendship—Fiction. 2. Drug abuse—Fiction]
I. Title.
PZ7.H79260n 1985   [Fic]   85-42632
ISBN 0-06-022598-X
ISBN 0-06-022599-8 (lib. bdg.)

Designed by Al Cetta
1 2 3 4 5 6 7 8 9 10
First Edition

To my father

Part One

Now tell me, are you experienced?
Have you ever been experienced?
Well . . . I have.
                                    —Jimi Hendrix

Chapter One

It was close to midnight when I got the phone call about Chris. I was facing my third all-nighter in less than a week, and I was only halfway through reading period. That's what they call the two weeks before college exams when you try to make up for a semester of goofing off.

When the phone rang, I was sitting in my room in front of my toaster-oven, staring through the little window at a frozen Macaroni and Cheese Supreme. I'd rather tell you I was in bed with some voluptuous coed, but my father keeps saying he sent me to college to "seek truth," so I won't bother spicing up the story. It was the end of my first semester, and I still didn't have a girlfriend. I wasn't even close, if you want to know the truth.

Back in high school, I used to dream of going off to college and living in coed dorms with half-naked girls floating up and down the hallways day and night. But the school I ended up at sticks all the freshman boys together in three grungy buildings. I'm kind of a slob myself, but these guys live like animals. The hall bathroom is such a sewer, you have to wear boots just to go in there and take a leak. That's an exaggeration, but believe me, it's gross.

Dorm life isn't all it's cracked up to be, let me tell you. Even my toaster-oven is illegal. But there's nowhere on campus to get food after midnight—which is when I'm usually hungry—so that night I was sitting there like a moron watching this macaroni cook. The frost had melted off the top, and if you stared real hard at it, you could see the cheese beginning to brown. What I was actually doing was stalling, because I had to read the entire *Canterbury Tales* that night. I'd already read them in eleventh grade, so I thought the Chaucer course would be a breeze. But it turns out that in college you have to read them in the original Middle English.

> *Whan that Aprille with his shoures soote,*
> *The droghte of March has perced to the roote.*

It might as well have been Swahili. It also turns out that the *Canterbury Tales* isn't just a bunch of funny, sexy stories. The first time I read them they were a scream. All these characters, some of them even priests, are fooling around with each other's wives and almost getting caught and having to climb out of windows with only half their clothes on. I was surprised to find that kind of stuff going on five hundred years ago. But according to my college professor the *Tales* were actually a critique of fourteenth-century Christianity, or else a proof of the existence of God, I can't remember which.

Well, that kind of killed Chaucer for me, so I put him on the back burner for the rest of the semester.

They keep the library open all night during reading period, but I hate that place. It was built by some nineteenth-century robber baron who probably never learned how to read, and it feels like a factory inside. You're not allowed to eat or smoke, and the fluorescent lights make this buzzing sound that gives me a headache. So I spent that reading period studying in my dorm room, which was starting to look more like a hamster cage, what with the notebooks and overflowing ashtrays and dirty laundry piled a foot deep on the floor. Since I came to college, my room is always a wreck. Probably a reaction to all those years of having my mom nag me to clean after myself.

The same with smoking. At home, I'd have to sneak outside to smoke a butt, then chew a stick of gum to hide the smell on my breath. My parents are both reformed smokers, which are the worst kind. My father, who's a doctor, was always giving me gory details about emphysema and lung cancer, about how your lungs turn black and shrivel up like prunes. That can really take the fun out of cigarettes. So when I got away to college, I started right in smoking like a fiend. I even pasted my empty Marlboro boxes in rows along the wall, like an Andy Warhol painting. But I took them down when I noticed all the dumb jocks building pyramids out of empty beer cans.

I spent my whole first semester doing everything I

wasn't allowed to do at home. Almost everything. You see, it turns out that college girls are allergic to freshman guys. No kidding. You can be at a party talking to a girl, and everything's going fine. Then you mention your freshman lit course, and—*whammo*—you're a ghost! She looks right through you like you're Claude Rains playing the Invisible Man. It was creepy the first time it happened, but after a while it's just depressing.

But that's a whole other story. I was telling you about those all-nighters during reading period. I wasn't using anything but coffee and cold showers to stay awake, but by the end of the week my mind had pretty much turned to mush. I just sat there in front of the toaster-oven, listening to my head ring.

"Hey, Kaufman!" someone shouted from the hallway. "If you're not too busy playing with yourself in there, your dad's on the phone."

Right away I knew something was wrong. My father never calls—only my mom. I mean, he'll pick up the upstairs extension and ask if I have enough money or clothes, but he never calls himself. My mom does that. And she always rings me at about seven in the morning with "I wanted to catch you before your first class"— even though she knows my first class isn't till nine-thirty, and I always sleep through breakfast. I guess she's just checking up on me, but I wish I could be somewhere else when she calls, just once.

I picked up the phone. "Hi, Dad."

"Did I wake you, Son?"

"No, I was just studying for my finals."

"Daniel . . . I'm afraid I have some bad news."

I didn't say anything. It always makes me nervous when he calls me Daniel, instead of just Danny.

"It's about your friend, Chris. He's had an accident."

I recognized the tone in his voice—the same one he uses with his patients' families.

"Is he going to be all right?" was all I could manage.

"We're doing all we can, but . . . he took a nasty fall. I hate to be the one to tell you about this, but your mother's too upset to talk to you right now."

"But he's alive, right?" One of my legs started shaking.

"There's only so much impact the cerebral cortex can sustain before the swelling—"

"C'mon, Dad, don't get technical on me."

Usually my father gets pissed off if I interrupt him, but he let it pass. "I don't think he's going to make it, Son."

Right then I had this image of my father holding the phone at the other end, waiting for me to say something.

"That's okay," I mumbled. It sounded real dumb as soon as it left my mouth. "How'd it happen?"

"You know that big tree on the golf course where you used to go sledding? It seems he was climbing around there last night . . . and fell."

"At night? In January? I don't get it."

"That's all they told me."

Then I got it. "He was wasted, right?"

"What?"

"He was stoned or fucked up on something, wasn't he?"

"I don't know the details." He sounded embarrassed. "We'll have to wait for the autopsy—if it comes to that. In any case, I thought you might want to come home."

"Yeah . . . I guess."

"I'll reimburse you for the train fare." He started in reciting arrival and departure schedules, but my mind was tearing off in a dozen directions.

"I'll see you tomorrow, Dad." After I hung up, I had to wait a minute for my leg to stop shaking.

Then the fire alarm went off with a piercing shriek, and everyone streamed out into the hallway. A plume of black smoke was pouring from my room—something in my toaster-oven had caught fire.

Chapter Two

The next morning I packed a bag and put on my dark-blue suit, which I hadn't worn since high school graduation. I figured it was easier to wear than to carry. I didn't bother saying good-bye to anyone before going to the train station. None of my college friends knew Chris, and I didn't feel like talking to them about it anyway. They weren't really close friends, and new friends aren't like old friends. You have to explain too much stuff.

I brought along the *Canterbury Tales* to read on the train, but I didn't even open it. I sat back and watched New Jersey roll by looking grayer and bleaker than usual, an endless line of dumpy little towns and spindly trees. Eventually I just closed my eyes and listened to the wheels move over the tracks. I hadn't seen Chris in several years, but he was right there when I shut my eyes. I wondered if he'd always seem that close.

I first met Chris when I transferred to Donnel School in the seventh grade. Only it was called the first form because Donnel was this really old-fashioned boys' day school outside Washington, D.C. It was even backward in the late sixties, which was when my parents decided I wasn't "fulfilling my potential" at public school.

Donnel was one of those places that molded men out of boys by dressing them up in jackets and ties and calling them by their last names. And if that didn't do the trick, football would. Everyone had to play. They even had an annual "Shrimp Bowl" between the third graders and the sixty-five-pound team. The teachers, called masters, were mostly retired military men who doubled as sports coaches. Sometimes it was hard to tell if you were in prep school or the army. Colonel Lathrop, my French teacher and football coach, began his first class by announcing, "If I could train ten thousand Orientals in guerrilla warfare, I can certainly teach you twenty boys French."

After lunch on the first day of school, the whole class emptied out into the main courtyard for a game of tie tag. I'd never played before, so I just followed along. Everyone took off his necktie and tucked it halfway into the back of his pants. Someone hollered "Go!" and the game was on. Eighty boys tore around in every direction trying to steal each other's ties. No teams or anything, just an every-man-for-himself free-for-all. The last one left with his tie was the winner.

Nobody paid much attention to me, the new kid on the block, and I was happy to hang around the fringes and watch the action. After the crowd thinned out, I moved in for a few easy grabs, always careful to keep my back to a wall. Pretty soon there were only a dozen players left. Then half a dozen. I kept darting around, avoiding face-offs and trying to stay alive. The guys who'd lost their ties were circled around us now, shouting encouragement. Finally, there were only three of us left. While the other two guys were going at it, I crept in behind one of them and yanked out his tie.

He whirled around with an angry glare. "Sneak," he hissed as he grabbed back his tie and sulked toward the sidelines.

I turned to face my opponent. The first thing I noticed about him was his shirt. Practically everyone wore white button-downs, but this guy's was bright red. He was smaller than me, but I could tell he was agile and quick, like a shortstop or a wide receiver. He sized me up the way the fox eyes the chicken in cartoons. His eyes were dark and bright, and he showed a lot of teeth through his wide smile—not smug exactly, but supremely confident. In his left hand he clutched a rainbow of neckties—there must have been twenty of them—dangling in the air like a fistful of snakes.

I was nervous as hell and just wanted to get through it without looking foolish. But he was in no hurry. Slowly, deliberately, he tucked in his shirttails so I'd have a clear shot at his tie. It seemed like a practiced ritual, so I did the same. Then he turned his back on me, real nonchalant, his tie hanging there for the taking. I knew it was a setup, so I made a few feints and dodges to try and turn him around. But he just stood there, very cool and collected, arranging the neckties in rows between his fingers. By this time the peanut gallery had started in with cries of "Do it!" and "Make your move!" which only made me edgier. But the gauntlet had been thrown down, and there was no escaping the challenge. I inched forward to within striking distance and poised for the attack. Then, just as I lunged, he spun deftly to his right and plucked my tie as I lurched past. It was one fluid gesture, graceful as a matador's—and I was the clumsy bull. When I turned to face him, he handed me my tie with a deep bow.

Then, before the crowd could respond, he sprinted through an archway and out of the courtyard, the other neckties still clutched in his fist. Everyone streamed out after him, shouting and screaming like a pack of hounds. I had my tie back, but I didn't want to miss out on the chase.

It was wild. The pack was in hot pursuit, but the fox had a big lead as he scampered out across the playing fields, the ties held defiantly overhead. He wove a course around the campus, turning back occasionally to hurl a laughing taunt. When we were finally gaining on him, he swerved sharply downhill and vaulted over the white picket fence guarding the headmaster's yard. We only hesitated a moment before clambering in after him.

There he was, dancing through the headmaster's orchard, scattering neckties on every tree. When he'd exhausted his supply of tinsel, he leaped the far fence and took off uphill again. As everyone scurried to retrieve their ties, I caught sight of him watching gleefully from atop the knoll.

It was only later that I understood why he got away with that kind of stunt, how his charm gave him license to behave outrageously and always be forgiven. All I knew then was I wanted to join him on that hilltop.

Chapter Three

It took me half an hour to reconstruct the neat Windsor my mother had knotted for me that morning. It was the only tie I owned, red with diagonal blue stripes, and I'd only worn it twice a year, at Thanksgiving and Passover.

By the time I straggled into English class, still fussing with the knot, Captain Parks was halfway through the roll. Parks, who'd once commanded a submarine in the South Pacific, barked out the names with military precision.

"Haufield."

"Here, sir."

"Howe."

"Here, sir."

"Jordan."

"Here . . . sir."

There he was—my tie-tag nemesis—calmly doodling away on the inside cover of his Norton Anthology. I slid into an empty desk beside him as Captain Parks glared up from his roll book.

"That shirt's not regulation, Jordan."

Jordan stared down at his shirt, then back at Parks. "No, sir, it's red."

Someone giggled.

"I run a tight ship here, Jordan. I won't have any impertinence—or red shirts."

"Aye aye, sir."

Jordan rose slowly to his feet and began unbuttoning his shirt. Oblivious of Parks's threatening scowl, he stripped down to a Superman T-shirt. The class erupted with laughter.

"Take a lap, Jordan," ordered Parks, jerking his thumb toward the playing field outside the window. Jordan sighed heavily and headed for the door, winking at me as he passed.

"Kaufman."

It was Captain Parks back at his roll call.

"Kaufman?" Louder this time, mispronouncing the first syllable. I hate it when people pronounce it *cowf* instead of *cough*.

"Here," I answered.

"Here what?" demanded Parks.

"Here, uh . . ." I hadn't caught on to the "sir" routine, which was mandatory when addressing a master.

"Here, *sir*, Kaufman."

"Here, sir. But it's pronounced *Kauf*man . . . sir."

"Take a lap, *Kauf*man."

By the time I got outside, he was already twenty yards ahead of me, loping along with graceful, effortless strides. I had to sprint to catch up to him.

He smiled when I came abreast of him. "What're you in for, bub?" he drawled like Bogart.

"I forgot to say 'sir.' "

"Men have fried for that." He laughed and reverted to his normal voice. "Forget it. Too nice a day to sit inside, anyway."

He veered off the field and ducked into a stand of pine trees. After a moment's pause, I followed. Somehow, he was already perched comfortably on a low-hanging bow, drawing a crumpled pack of Camel nonfilters from his jacket pocket.

"Won't they be looking for us?" I asked, immediately sorry for sounding so wimpy.

"Don't worry about Parks. He's been shell-shocked since the war. Want a smoke?"

I shook my head. "I'm trying to lay off . . . for sports."

Actually, I wasn't smoking yet, and I sure didn't want to get caught at it my first day of school. What was I doing here in the bushes anyway?

"Yeah, it's bad for the old bellows, but what the hell." He pulled a mangled cigarette from the pack and straightened it between two fingers. "You're new, right?"

I nodded. "My name's Kaufman . . . Danny."

He lit up, holding his gaze on me as he exhaled a tight column of smoke. "Chris Jordan," he said finally. "Good to have some new blood around here."

I felt a rush of happy relief. "Are they all as bad as Parks?" was all I could think to ask.

"Some are a lot worse. Y'know, really into humiliation

[15]

tactics. Parks just likes to keep things shipshape. But you have to goose these guys once in a while, or they'll drive you nuts."

"But don't you get in trouble?"

"Laps, study hall—what can they do to me? Without us here to kick around, they're out of work."

"I never thought of it that way."

"No one does, but we're gonna change all that." He stubbed out the butt and sprang to his feet. "In the meantime, you should find yourself a friend. Around here, you'll be needing one."

And with that he was off, running out along the perimeter of the field on his way back to Captain Parks's tight ship. And I was right behind him.

Chapter Four

We didn't shake on it or anything, but that was the beginning of our alliance. It was us against the world, or at least the world as represented by Donnel School. And the masters weren't the only enemies. That place was a snake pit—everything was competitive, setting one student against another. You were graded and ranked in each subject every quarter, and the grades were posted outside the headmaster's office, so you'd know exactly who was ahead of you or sneaking up behind. And that was just the academic side of it. In sports there was always an A team, a B team, and a C team. And if you messed up on the field, the coach would nail you for it the next morning in French class. "You conjugate a verb about as well as you tackle, Kaufman."

Since most of the masters seated their students alphabetically, Jordan and Kaufman sat side by side in four classes. Chris was always trying to crack me up with his doodled caricatures, and since I was sort of a brain in those days, I'd help him through pop quizzes, whispering answers to him if he got caught napping. It's not that Chris was dumb—he was always dreaming up brilliant pranks—but he never took any interest in books. "Dead trees," he called them. For Chris, classes were just a way of passing the time till sports practice.

On the playing field Chris had no equal. He was one of those total "naturals" who couldn't drop a pass or miss a basketball hoop. And he was faster than the wind. It would have been obnoxious in someone else, but Chris managed to make everyone look good. He'd just appear under any pass, no matter how poorly thrown, and when he tackled someone it looked like a ballet move that they'd been rehearsing together for weeks. It's one thing watching pro atheletes pull those kinds of moves on television; but when it happens right in front of you, on your own puny field—damn, it's beautiful!

After football practice, he and I would stay late running plays. Chris had this idea I should try out for quarterback. I'd just as soon have stayed on the defensive line, where the coach put me, but Chris wanted us to play on offense together.

"You've definitely got the arm for it," he insisted. "Your only problem is confidence. That's all McNair has over you. That and a few years' experience. But believe me, you can take him anytime you want."

Bill McNair wasn't just the starting quarterback. He was also the meanest asshole in the first form. You know, the kind of guy who picks on someone in the locker room by pointing at his dick and yelling, "They don't make jockstraps in your size, Haufield. Better try a training bra." That sort of thing. And if he ever took on someone tough, McNair made sure that Laird was somewhere nearby. Phil Laird, McNair's buddy and the biggest guy in the class, was known by everyone as Sherman, as in Sherman tank. Laird played on the offensive line with the other big lunks who protected the quarterback. Off the field he served pretty much the same function.

Chris and I were running pass patterns after practice one day when the two of them sauntered out of the gym and studied us from the sidelines.

McNair nudged Laird. "Look at that," he said in a loud voice. "Jordan and the Jew. Some combo, huh? Jordan can even make a kike look good."

I forgot to mention that out of eighty first formers, there were only two Jews and one black kid, who happened to be the son of the Nigerian ambassador and a ringer of a soccer player. That's the kind of school it was. The other Jewish guy was Bobby Meyers, the class nerd and chairman of the stamp club, so naturally I steered clear of him. Ever since school began, McNair had been needling me with little digs like "Hope you invite me to your Fart Mitzvah," but I'd done my best to ignore him. McNair wasn't the sort of guy you wanted to tangle with when you were just starting out somewhere. Anyway, I never mentioned it to Chris, and McNair had been careful not to make any of his wisecracks in front of him.

I lofted a spiral toward Chris, hoping he hadn't heard this one—but he had. He stood stock-still, staring at McNair, while the ball sailed over his head and fell into the dirt. It wasn't like Chris to miss a pass. It made me nervous, and McNair didn't look too relaxed himself.

Chris tossed aside his helmet and walked up to the two of them, real slow. "What was that you said? I missed it."

"He said you even make the Jewboy look good," answered Laird in his big dumb voice.

"I meant it as a compliment," offered McNair. He hadn't expected Chris to take offense, and he sure didn't want to cross his best receiver.

"That's funny," said Chris, "it didn't sound to me like a compliment."

"Hey, forget it," I said lamely. I didn't want him fighting my battles.

Chris stepped right up to McNair, almost touching him now. "Sherman here is too stupid to know any better. But I'm surprised to hear you talk that way. Don't you know I'm Jewish?"

"With a name like Jordan?" It was Laird talking, but I was thinking the same thing.

"My dad changed it from Jordanowitz—for professional reasons. Any objections?"

McNair squirmed under his stare. "It was just a crack. I didn't mean anything by it."

"Well, me and Kaufman don't want to hear that shit. So keep it to yourself." And with that Chris turned his back and walked away.

What happened next was pretty amazing. I should explain that penny loafers were an unofficial part of the Donnel uniform. And it was fashionable to break down the backs of your loafers so you could slip in and out of them easily. Guys were always kicking their shoes high in the air, then running to catch them. But I'd never seen them used as weapons.

As Chris was walking away, I saw Laird cock his right foot and rocket a loafer straight for his head. There wasn't time to shout a warning—but I didn't need to. Somehow, Chris felt it coming, like the sheriff who senses the saloon gunslinger drawing behind his back. As he spun around, his hand reached up instinctively to catch the missile as it flew by his ear. Just like that—like he'd called for a pitch in that exact spot.

Everyone was stunned, including me. Laird backed away, braced for the return volley. But it never came. Instead, Chris clamped his teeth firmly on the edge of the loafer's sole, and with a savage tear of the hand, he ripped it off the shoe. Then he opened his jaws and let it drop in the dust.

Laird just stood there too shocked to respond, till McNair finally grabbed his elbow and led him away. Laird hobbled off, but not without a sad glance back at his shredded shoe.

"You never told me you were Jewish," I said when they had gone.

"I'm not." He shrugged. "Let's try a post pattern."

He hiked me the ball and raced downfield. I threw a wobbly pass, which he somehow managed to get under and catch.

Chapter Five

I'd never had a best friend before, someone I knew was really on my side. It made everything okay, even the bad stuff, because now I had someone to share it with. What used to be boring or scary was suddenly an adventure. And if anything went wrong, I knew that one of us could always figure a way out. It made me feel a lot older.

It seems like we spent all our time together that fall. If we went back to my house after school, my mom was always looking in on us. Or else my little brother, Mark, would be hanging around. But Chris was an only child and both his parents worked, so we had his place to ourselves all afternoon. The only person there was Nellie, their maid, but she was usually busy doing the ironing and watching wrestling on TV. We could hear her in the next room, cheering on her current favorite or cursing his opponent with bloodcurdling cries. "Break that bad man's head open! Shake his brains loose!"

Besides the privacy, the best thing about the Jordans' house was playing with the high-tech appliances. Chris's father was a big-shot corporate lawyer who always bought the latest gadgets—trash compactors, ice makers, remote-control garage doors, you name it. So first off we'd raid the self-defrosting, double-doored refrigerator that was stocked with fancy deli food wrapped in white waxed paper. Then down we'd go to the refinished basement to eat our snack in front of the remote-control color television.

We'd usually watch *Wheel It or Deal It*, a really moronic game show where you'd have to decide between spinning the money wheel or trading your spin for a hidden box filled with either riches or garbage. The studio audience went crazy, shrieking "Wheel It!" or "Deal It!" and the host was this greasy old guy who liked to feel up the women contestants. It was a stupid show all right, but we like to watch anyway. You see, we were sort of in love with the girls who stood onstage pointing at the mystery boxes. Maybe love wasn't the word for it, but they were really something. There were three of them—a blonde, a brunette, and a redhead, one for each box—and they each wore a shiny miniskirt and a totally knowing smile, like her box held the best prize you could possibly imagine. They never said a word, and I can't remember their names, but the way they smiled kept me up at night.

But our favorite program was *The Time Tunnel*. It was about these two guys who were caught in time, and every week they'd find themselves at some key point in history right before a catastrophe was scheduled to happen. Like aboard the *Titanic* just ahead of the iceberg, or in Pompeii forty-five minutes before the volcano was due to blow. Every week they'd try to avert the disaster before it happened. But of course they never could, so they'd end up scurrying back to the time tunnel at the end of the show, just as the roof was caving in. Only along the way one of them always fell in love with Helen of Troy or some other doomed chick. So his buddy would have to remind him that "You can't change history" and drag him back to the tunnel, leaving his heart behind in the third century B.C. or wherever. That was sort of the moral of the show—"You can't change history"—and it seemed like one of the guys would repeat that line every episode. Their other problem was that the time tunnel was on the fritz. They were trapped inside, condemned to roam through time, week after week, till the scientists back in the present could figure out how to bring them home.

"I'd trade places with them in a minute," declared Chris one day, when the dynamic duo had escaped from Little Big Horn after failing to convince Custer that Crazy Horse was on the warpath. "They're always where the action is."

"Yeah, but they're never gonna get home."

"That's the best part. Imagine if you never had to mow the lawn again, never had to wash your father's car or listen to his dumb rules."

"And never had to play football?" I thought I had him there.

"You think we invented sports or something? What about the ancient Olympic games? Now there was real competition. Or how about racing a chariot around the Colosseum with half a million Romans cheering you on?"

"And if you lose you get thrown to the lions."

"The point is," he explained impatiently, "in just about any other period of history we wouldn't be wasting our lives sitting in classrooms or in front of television sets. We'd be young men out in the world—fighting wars, seducing women, building empires. You know, the real stuff."

"But this is real."

"No it's not," he snapped back angrily. "This is bullshit. This is following orders and killing time. Don't you see that?" He was really worked up now. "You don't get it, do you? Wait a minute."

He reached down below the stereo cabinet and pulled out an album with great ceremony.

"Check this out, man," he said excitedly as he laid the needle down on the spinning disc. "It'll blow you away."

I owned a few Beatles records, but this didn't sound like anything I'd ever heard before. It had electric guitars that sounded more like rockets flying through space. And the voices were dreamy and far away, as if you were hearing them through a wall of water.

I looked at the album, titled *The Jimi Hendrix Experience*. The jacket featured a distorted photo of the group, shot through a fish-eye lens, like they use in the movies to show someone's dreaming or drunk. The lead guitarist, Jimi Hendrix, was this wild-looking black dude with a huge Afro. He was flanked by two white guys—the drummer and the bass player.

Chris cranked up the volume full blast, till the whole room started to shake with sound. "Just sit back and let it wash over you," he instructed.

The music was everywhere, and the high-pitched lead guitar sort of slid inside me as the refrain to the title song echoed in my head:

> *Now tell me, are you experienced?*
> *Have you ever been experienced?*
> *We-e-e-ell, I-I-I-I have.*

He kept repeating that question in a low, seductive voice—a very personal question. I wasn't sure what kind of experience he was referring to, but I knew I hadn't had it. Whatever it was, he made it sound choice.

"What do you think he means, 'experienced'?" I asked when the record was over.

"Y'know, sex. Or else drugs. I'm not sure which."

"What drugs?"

"Marijuana, I guess."

"That's what I thought."

All I knew about drugs back then was from a cover story in *Life* magazine about the hippies in San Francisco. They dropped out of college, wore bright-colored clothes, and spent all day picking flowers and taking drugs. But that was happening three thousand miles away to people ten years older than me. I tried to imagine what would happen if I turned up in Captain Parks's class wearing torn jeans and holding a bouquet of daisies. He'd have me running laps the rest of my life.

"Maybe we should try to get some of that stuff," ventured Chris.

"What stuff?"

"Marijuana."

"But isn't that illegal?"

"Sure, but all the best things are."

"Yeah? Like what?"

He had to think a minute. "Like sex, for instance. Did you know if you screw a girl under sixteen, they can send you to jail?"

"Are you sure about that?"

"My dad says they can. It's called statuary rape."

I wasn't in any immediate danger of incarceration, but still, that came as discouraging news.

"The point is," he continued, "sometimes you have to break the rules. Look at the Boston Tea Party. That was illegal."

"Yeah, but that wasn't a real party. It was the beginning of a revolutionary war."

"That's what I'm talking about."

I didn't think I was ready to break the law, much less go to jail. But I didn't tell Chris that. Instead, I picked up the album and studied the picture again. There was Jimi Hendrix—even the name was weird—staring straight at me with that knowing look in his eyes. No doubt about it, this guy was definitely experienced. He was just about the most experienced person I'd ever seen.

Chapter Six

Our football team was rolling through the season with an undefeated record. But then, as our coach reminded us before each game, Donnel's honor was at stake. The masters brought all their military training to their coaching roles. The gridiron was their field of battle, and we were the footsoldiers in their elaborate campaigns. Victory was the only acceptable outcome.

One day after practice, Captain Lathrop pulled Chris aside for a chat. I couldn't hear what he was saying, but it was obviously bad news. Chris just stared down at the ground and pawed the dirt with his cleats.

"Well, that's the season," he announced when he caught up with me in the showers.

"What's the problem?"

"If I don't pass my midterm tomorrow," he said, bowing his head under the steaming water, "Lathrop has to put me on the ineligible list."

Donnel was very serious about the old athlete-scholar ideal. If you were flunking a course at midterm, you became ineligible for sports for the rest of the semester. But I couldn't believe Lathrop would flunk his star player.

"But you said Lathrop was passing you in French."

"*Français, oui.*" He shut off the shower for emphasis. "Latin, *non.*"

In keeping with its classical self-image, Donnel was one of the last schools in the country that required three years of Latin. They believed that any truly educated young man should be fluent in a language no one had spoken for a thousand years. I think that's why my father was so hot to send me to Donnel.

"I'd never have made it through first-year anatomy without Latin" was his standard response to my gripes. Doctors still use Latin names for body parts, and my father hoped I'd follow in his medical footsteps. Fat chance of that. I once went to watch my father take out an appendix. The minute his scalpel touched flesh, I passed out cold. An orderly had to carry me out of the operating room.

"I was thinking," Chris mused as we walked to the bus, "maybe I could write the verb conjugations on the inside of my necktie."

"If they catch you cheating on a midterm, you're finished."

"That's the only way I'll pass."

"How about studying for a change?"

"But the test's tomorrow morning. The Latins didn't build Rome in a day, you know."

"That still leaves tonight. I'll come over after dinner."

When I showed up at Chris's, he was stretched out on the basement couch watching *Star Trek*. "You're just in time," he said, barely looking up from the tube. "The

Klingons have surrounded the *Enterprise* and Kirk's about to—"

I clicked off the set. "You can catch the reruns. It's time to get down to work."

Chris rolled over on the couch. "I appreciate the effort, old buddy, but it's an exercise in futility."

"I've made up a list of seventy nouns and verbs we may have to decline and conjugate," I continued in a businesslike manner. "I figure if we do ten an hour, we can knock off at three in the morning."

By midnight we'd only covered a dozen words and our eyelids were getting heavier by the minute. There was a gentle knock and Chris's mom poked her head in the doorway carrying a tray of cookies and milk. Mrs. Jordan was a pretty, delicate woman who always seemed sort of frightened, like she was afraid you were going to yell at her.

"I'll just set these down and let you boys get on with your work."

"Thanks, Mrs. Jordan," I said, grabbing a handful of cookies.

"Please call me Kitty," she asked in her tinkerbell voice.

"Okay . . . Kitty." I never felt comfortable calling people's parents by their first names, and "Kitty" sounded so girlish—not at all like a mother.

"I'll be back in a minute," said Chris as he got up and scooted out of the room.

Mrs. Jordan watched him leave, then leaned forward

and whispered, "Chris told me about your predicament. I hope he can help you through it."

"*My* predicament?" I whispered back. Why was I whispering?

"I know how tough foreign languages can be," she continued sympathetically. "And I hear you're a great asset to the football team."

"Oh . . . yeah." It was all coming clear now. "But I'm sure with Chris's help I'll make out all right."

Just then Chris returned and sidled up to his mother. They were about the same height, and looking at them side by side, I noticed how alike they were: same eyes, same mouth and nose. She instinctively laid her hand on his head, as if he were still a small boy, and you could tell that he didn't mind, that he liked it when she ran her fingers through his hair.

"Don't work too hard now, boys," she said as she tip-toed out of the room.

When she'd gone, I glared over at Chris. "So I'm flunking Latin, am I?"

"If they knew *I* was, they'd kill me—or cut off my allowance, anyway."

"So I get to play the dunce. Thanks."

"Don't mention it." He smiled. "Check these out." He opened his hand to reveal two capsules. They looked like time-release cold pills.

"What are they?"

He grinned mischeivously. "Study aids."

"But I don't have a cold."

"They're not for colds, they're for dieting."

"Are we trying to lose weight?"

"No. But we can stay up all night with these."

I eyed the two capsules skeptically. "Those are gonna help us conjugate verbs?"

"Sure. College students use them all the time."

"Where'd you get 'em?"

"From my mom's medicine cabinet. She's got a whole bottle full."

I didn't want to seem like a wimp, and I *was* sleepy. So I shrugged my consent, and we swallowed them down with milk.

We pushed on, struggling gamely through some more verbs. About an hour later we were at *vincere*—to win.

"*Vincere—vinco, vincis, vincit*," I instructed.

"*Vinco, vincis, vincit*," parroted Chris.

"*Vinco, vincis, vincit*," I repeated.

"*Vinco, vincis, vincit?*" he asked.

"*Vinco-vincis-vincit*," I answered back.

They were just sounds strung together like stones on a necklace. Funny sounds that made us want to laugh out loud. So we did. It was just so funny—conjugating verbs from a dead language in the middle of the night so we could chase a lopsided ball around a playing field. Some things you just have to laugh at.

We flew through the imperatives. Past perfect? No problem. Our minds were racing a mile a minute, and so were our tongues. Even Chris was whipping along at chariot speed. . . . *amas, amat, amamus . . . Sum, esse, fui*. He sounded like a Caesar.

It was amazing. Our minds opened up like accordions—no, like giant sponges soaking up oceans full of data. We coasted downhill at eighty miles an hour without even pedaling—just held on tight to the handlebars and flew. We even had time to compose a song along the way—"The Ballad of Cicero," sung to the tune of "Hey Jude." It went something like this:

> *Hey Cicero, don't make it sad*
> *Amas veritas will make it better,*
> *Remember, sic transit under your skin,*
> *Then you'll begin*
> *Sum esse fui, to Latin.*

We were on the third verse when we noticed it was light outside. And we weren't even tired.

"Just think," exclaimed Chris, his eyes wide as saucers, "we may never have to sleep again. We could start a secret society—the Nightcrawlers. While the rest of the world sleeps, we'll be up plotting the revolution!"

"In Latin!"

"In Pig Latin—the extinct language of ancient swine. No one will be able to decipher our messages."

"Except the pigs."

"Pigs of the world unite—you have nothing to lose but your sties!"

Kitty peeked in the room. "You boys still up?"

"Naturally," said Chris with an expansive sweep of his arm. "You think we can study in our sleep?" That cracked us up.

Kitty made us breakfast. We couldn't eat a bite, but the sight of those eggs staring up at us was a scream.

I was still going strong on the bus ride to school. "Just think if we never had to sleep *or* eat," I said. "We'd be a new race of super androids, playing football all night, calling the signals in Latin. Or Greek! What about Greek?"

I waited for Chris to second my brilliant suggestion, but he was passed out cold on the seat beside me.

"Hey, look alive!" I shouted too loudly, attracting attention from the other bus riders. "We've still got to *ass-pay* the *est-tay*," I whispered in my best Pig Latin.

I shook him till he sputtered awake.

"—Huh? Oh—what a horrible dream. I was being eaten by a chicken—a fried chicken!"

"Forget the chicken. Let's practice some verbs."

"The test—oh my god—I forgot!"

"Be cool. We'll warm up with an easy one—*esse*. Piece of cake."

"*Esse?* What's that?"

"To be," I reminded him, struggling to contain my panic. "Now conjugate it."

He furrowed his brow. "I can't."

"Sure you can."

"No, I can't."

"What do you mean, you can't? You had it down cold an hour ago."

"Seems like last month," he said groggily.

"To be—*sum, esse, fui*," I prompted.

"To be . . . *su* . . . *sun* . . . *sunes*—I can't. It's gone."

I grabbed his head with both hands and shook. "It can't be gone. It's got to be in there someplace!"

"Maybe last night, but now . . ." He shrugged and nodded back to sleep.

I couldn't believe it. I kept waiting for some fairy godmother to send an awakening snowfall, like in *The Wizard of Oz*. But we were nowhere near the Emerald City. In fact, the bus was arriving at school.

I shook Chris awake again.

"You remember our song, don't you?" I led him through the first verse of "Hey Cicero," By the end of the second verse he had joined in on his own. We were getting some funny looks from the other kids on the bus, but we were beyond caring about them. When we finished the song, I took him through it again. It seemed to help. A few of the verbs came back to him, but he was still shaky.

Latin was our first class, so we cut homeroom and headed straight for the gym, which was deserted that time of day. We stripped off our clothes and jumped into the showers with all the jets turned on cold. That put the lights back in our eyes. For the next twenty minutes we stood there in the cold shower, hollering verbs back and forth like a couple of lunatics.

Our hair was still dripping water when we got to Latin class. The master, Mr. Wilbur, stopped handing out the exams when we walked in.

"Mr. Jordan, you may sit here," he commanded, directing Chris to a desk in the front row. "And you, Mr. Kaufman, may occupy that desk." He pointed to one in the rear of the class.

That got me feeling pretty paranoid, let me tell you. Was he onto us? Had he infiltrated the Secret Society of Hogs? Everyone knew we were best friends, but still . . .

I don't remember much about the exam, except that I had trouble keeping my eyes focused on the page. They kept zeroing in on different spots—the tip of my eraser, the fingernail of my left pinky, the large black fly that was circling the room. I kept checking to see if Chris was still awake, and a few times I caught him rapping his forehead with his fist—I mean really smacking himself good. And once I thought I heard someone humming "Hey Jude" but it might have been me.

"Pencils up, gentlemen," commanded Mr. Wilbur, signaling the end of the exam. I wasn't finished yet, but I was glad to have it over with. We staggered outside and slumped to the ground behind the old stone DONNEL SCHOOL sign.

"Well, what d'ya think, partner?" I asked.

"I think we ought to leave Latin to the pigs."

"But did you pass?"

"*eats-Bay e-may*," he mumbled, and fell asleep.

A minute later I was passed out next to him. We didn't come around till after lunch.

Then we had to wait all weekend for the verdict. Monday morning we rushed to the headmaster's office and peered up at the grade list posted on the door. The exam was graded on a curve, which meant the bottom ten percent of the class flunked. We started hopefully at the top of the list and worked our way down. I got in safely with a 78. Chris was already groaning in anticipation as we inched downward toward damnation. Then we found him—Jordan: 67—perched just above the dreaded red failure line.

"All right!" I shouted, pounding him joyously on the back.

"Piece of cake." He shrugged, but he was grinning like a goddamn Cheshire cat.

Chapter Seven

The football season was drawing to a close. Our final contest was the traditional Army–Navy game between the first and second formers. But it was as much a rivalry between the coaches as the players, with Colonel Lathrop commanding our Army squad and Captain Parks at the Navy helm. According to tradition, the older Navy team should stomp Army, or else suffer humiliation and ridicule the rest of the year.

But Colonel Lathrop was hopeful of an upset, what with our undefeated record and standout wide receiver. Chris was also the team captain, so it fell to him to deliver the formal challenge at the Middle School assembly. It was a pretty corny ritual, but he managed to breathe some life into it.

"On behalf of my comrades in the glorious Army of the First Form, I hearby challenge the rusted-out Navy team to show up for its post-season football lesson at Stoddard Stadium this Friday afternoon."

All the first formers pounded their feet in thunderous applause. Then the captain of the Navy team rose slowly to his feet. This guy was a real monster. He was so big, he made Sherman look undernourished.

"If you pussies dare to show up on Friday, we'll bury you ten feet under the field." The second formers hooted their approval. They were smug bastards.

A freezing rain was falling the day of the game, and all the players were standing around with their hands in their pants. For some reason, athletes are allowed to do that. You touch yourself down there when you're wearing street clothes and people think you're crude. But put on a sports uniform, and you can handle your jewels to your heart's content. Even the pros do it on television in front of coast-to-coast audiences. Like when the batter steps up to the plate and knocks the dirt out of his cleats, you just know he's gonna rearrange his crotch before the first pitch. It's like some damn religion with batters.

Anyway, we were standing around in the rain, waiting for the game to start. There wasn't much of a crowd, on account of the weather, but I was looking around to see if my father had shown up. Not being much of a sports fan, he hadn't come to any of our games that season. But that morning at breakfast he'd surprised me.

"I thought I'd drop by and catch your big game today," he said matter-of-factly.

I didn't look up from my plate of chicken livers, which is what my mom always served me the morning of a game.

"I was supposed to remove a patient's gallstones this afternoon," he explained, carefully folding his paper napkin the way he did after every meal. "But her astrologer tells her the moon's in the wrong house, or some such foolishness. I can't see what the moon should matter to a gallstone."

"Look who's talking," my mother chimed in from her position at the stove. "Whose prostate was inflamed so bad he could hardly pass water, but wouldn't let his partner operate on a Friday because it happened to be the thirteenth?"

My father dismissed her with a backhand wave. "Totally different issue. My partner plays golf every Friday afternoon of his life, come hail or sleet. I didn't want him rushing through my prostate on his way to the first tee."

He looked back to me. "So, what do you say? Could you use an extra fan?"

"Okay . . . if you want to," I mumbled without enthusiasm. Actually, I wasn't too hot on the idea. My father believed in "the pursuit of excellence," and I had the sinking feeling that the second formers were going to be displaying most of the excellence that afternoon.

The only person who thought we could win was Chris. He was bouncing up and down on the sidelines, trying to psych us up for the battle.

"These guys are flabby! We can take 'em in a walk. The bigger they come, the harder they fall!"

They were big all right, but they didn't do much falling the first half. Their huge front line kept us stacked up in the middle, and their pass rush was awesome. McNair got sacked a dozen times, and the ball was so wet he could hardly throw a spiral. To make matters worse, the field was so muddy that you couldn't tell the jerseys apart. Luckily, the mud slowed them down too, so they were only ahead 7–0 by the end of the first half.

During halftime we sucked on oranges and licked our wounds while Coach Lathrop lectured us on "internal fortitude."

"You think this mud is bad? When I was in Korea, we fought in the middle of monsoons. We had to march through swamps up to our waists, and there were leeches sucking our blood every step of the way. I don't see any leeches on this field, do you?" That cheered us up plenty, let me tell you.

But when they kicked off to start the second half, Chris caught the ball and raced down the sideline all the way to their ten-yard line. On the next play, McNair passed to Chris in the end zone. But we missed the extra point and still trailed 7–6.

Not much else happened till the middle of the fourth quarter. They were marching toward our goal line when suddenly the quarterback fumbled. Everyone scrambled for the ball while it shot around like a greased watermelon. Finally, it landed with a plop in the mud in front of me. I fell on it, and immediately eleven second formers piled on, kneeing and elbowing for the ball. But I held on.

It was really no big deal, but everyone was slapping my back and hooting, "Way t'go!" Even the coach called out, "Heads-up play, Kaufman," as I trotted to the sidelines. I looked around for my father, but he still hadn't arrived. Then I saw him walking up from the road under his black umbrella. My father, who's never late for anything, had missed my moment of glory. It figured.

Now our bench was all excited. We actually had a chance to win. Lathrop stomped up and down the muddy sideline, hollering through the rain like Captain Ahab railing against Moby Dick.

We managed to pull off a reverse, which got us to midfield. On the next play, McNair dropped back to pass, but their linebackers were blitzing. The two of them came charging in as McNair backpedaled frantically, searching for a receiver. Before he could unload the ball, one of them grabbed his legs while the other flew for his head. It was terrible to watch. McNair's helmet went flying and his body got twisted around like a corkscrew. I don't know how he held on to the ball.

The linebackers jumped to their feet and pounded each other's shoulders, but McNair just lay there in the mud, a mangled mess. I felt sorry for the guy, even if he was a first-class schmuck. They had to carry him off the field.

The two-minute warning sounded. We were down by a point, sixty yards from the goal line with time running out—and no quarterback. Just then the rain started coming down in torrents. Chris trotted over to the sideline to confer with Coach Lathrop. The coach kept shaking his head, but Chris stayed on him till he finally waved me over from the bench.

"Jordan here tells me you've played quarterback before. That right?"

"Well . . . actually—"

"I'm telling you he's a ringer," Chris cut in. "A great ball handler and an arm like Broadway Joe."

Lathrop was still dubious, but he didn't have many options. "Okay, Kaufman, you're in at quarterback. It's too wet to pass, so just keep it on the ground and try to get us into field-goal range." He gave me the ceremonial slap on the rump and sent me onto the field.

Let me tell you, my heart was ready to burst through my shoulderpads. I knew the plays all right—Chris had run me through the playbook every day for a month—but this was different. Suddenly there were ten guys huddled around, waiting for me to tell them what to do.

"Let's try a sweep left with the guards pulling," I said with as much authority as I could muster.

"When do I hike the ball, Moses?" It was Laird, the center. I'd forgotten to give the signal.

"On three."

The sweep didn't work. Neither did the next play, a slant off tackle. So it was third down and eight.

"We've got to try a pass play," said Chris as we walked back to the huddle.

"But the coach said—"

"Forget that. We've got to get into field-goal range."

He smiled across the huddle at me while I tried to keep my voice steady. "We're gonna do a pass. Ends line up tight. Jordan split wide right and run a post pattern. I'll look for you in the far corner." It seemed like I should add something inspirational, but all I could think to say was "Hike on two."

I surveyed the field as we went to the line. It was one big mud puddle and the rain wouldn't let up. I tried to dry my hands on my jersey, but it was hopeless. Nothing to do but run the play. I stepped up behind the center and barked out the signals.

"Set—hutt one—hutt two—"

The ball snapped back to me, slicker than a wet fish. I grasped it with both hands and dropped back into the pocket. Someone broke through the line and headed straight at me. I dodged left, and he sailed past. Now the whole front line was caving in. I couldn't spot Chris through the rain, but I knew where he should be. So I reared back and heaved the ball as far as I could in that direction.

The minute the ball left my hand, I knew it was trouble. It slipped off my fingers and headed off for the wrong corner. I wanted to push the stop-action button, reverse the play, and throw the ball over again. But it was gone.

Someone decked me, and by the time I got to my feet their linebacker had intercepted the pass and was running back up the sideline with nothing but open field ahead of him. Suddenly, out of nowhere, Chris flew across the field and flattened the guy with a vicious blind-side tackle. The ball spurted out from under him, and one of our guys recovered.

Now we had the ball on their twenty-yard line with fifteen seconds to play. Chris called time out, and our field-goal kicker trotted onto the field. It was still a long kick, especially in the rain, but we only had time for one more play.

The quarterback is the guy who holds the ball for the place kicker. I'd never done it before, but I'd watched it a thousand times on television. Looked simple enough. I lined up seven yards behind the center and crouched on one knee in the mud.

"Hutt one, hutt two, hutt three—"

The ball came sailing back, high. I managed to haul it in and place it down cleanly, spinning the laces toward the goal post. But as the kicker approached the ball, his back foot slipped out from under him and he flipped over backward, like Charlie Brown does in the comics. I froze there—kneeling in the mud with the ball as ten giant linemen stampeded toward me.

"Run it!" someone shouted. But there was nowhere to run. There were just these huge Navy assassins bearing down on me, shrieking as they came. While I tried to think, my legs backpedaled furiously in the direction of my own goal line. That's when I spotted Chris. He was alone in their end zone waving his hands wildly in the air. I threw the ball and prayed.

It wasn't a spiral, but it lofted over the onrushing jerseys and sailed toward the goal line. The wind caught the pass and was carrying it out of bounds when Chris made a desperate, yet graceful dive—a classic Jordan manuever—and snared the ball in the corner of the end zone.

Everyone went wild, of course. They mobbed me.

They mobbed Chris. We mobbed each other. The whole team rolled around in the mud together. It was great.

When it was all over, my father found me in the crowd. He had this big grin on his face, and he wrapped an arm around me even though I got mud all over his suit.

"That was an excellent pass, Son," he said into my ear. That really got me.

It was one of those moments you just want to seal up in a bottle, for keeps, so you can take it out on bad days and remember how great you felt that one time.

Chapter Eight

There was almost a month between the end of the football season and the beginning of basketball. Deprived of his only socially acceptable outlet, Chris put most of his energy into designing and executing pranks, what he called his "extracurricular activities." Silly stuff, really, like planting dry ice in trash cans so someone would pull the fire alarm in the middle of study hall. Or, once, he made up a fake grade list and posted it outside the headmaster's office. Of course on Chris's list all the perennial brains flunked out and the class dunces made first honor roll. You'd be amazed how upset some people got about that one.

He never got caught in the act, but it was pretty much common knowledge who was behind those stunts. Chris was fired up, and it must have been infectious, because pretty soon there were other pranksters at work—making joke announcements over the P.A. system, turning back clocks so the bell sequence got messed up, that sort of thing. This was the beginning of a general uprising, Chris believed. Soon the students would be ready for bolder actions, along the lines of college students on campuses all across the country—student strikes, building takeovers, etc.

But Donnel School wasn't about to be taken over by rebel students. Not as long as Paul Donnel Hatfield was in charge. Hatfield, the headmaster and founder of the school, was about a hundred years old and starting to show his age, but he never let you forget who was boss. You'd always see him touring the campus in his electric golf cart, pointing out pieces of litter for students to pick up or bawling them out for wearing their neckties loosened. He was a regular feature at football games, where he liked to lead the crowd in the school anthem— "Donnel Forever," to the tune of "America the Beautiful"—thrashing the air with his cane like a crazed orchestra conductor. Hatfield was one of those old people whose face had settled into a permanent scowl and who spoke primarily in grunts and snarls. Maybe he was just pissed off about growing old, but you got the feeling he'd always been that way.

Hatfield showed up unannounced at the next school assembly. Mr. Stoddard, the Middle School principal, had just finished telling us about the festivities planned for the school's fiftieth anniversary that month. There were going to be speeches, a banquet, the works. And we were all expected to pitch in and help make this gala event a success. With hundreds of visitors on campus that day, we'd all be responsible for making sure the grounds were spotless.

After Stoddard finished, Hatfield climbed up on the stage and rapped his cane on the podium, just to make sure we all knew he was there. Then he spent about five minutes clearing his throat, right into the microphone. It was pretty gross. When he was done, he glared down at us with this disgusted expression on his face, like he was looking into a refrigerator full of rotten food.

"You know what I see here in front of me?" he growled. "A bunch of long-haired J.D.s," meaning juvenile delinquents. "I'm not running a school for holligans. If you want to act like animals, you can go live in the jungle."

He slowly scanned the assembly, daring someone to cough or snicker.

"Let me tell you men something: Your mistakes follow you through life like a tail—a tail of shame. The more you screw up, the longer your tail grows. And it's not something you can hide like a pimple on your ass. It sticks out there for the whole world to see. So unless you want to crawl through life like goddamn crocodiles, I suggest you shape up, and fast."

He signaled Stoddard with his cane, then turned back to us with his best impersonation of a smile.

"Since I'm responsible for minding your tails, I've arranged—at my own expense—to make you presentable for our upcoming festivities. This anniversary means a lot to all of us here, and I want you looking like gentlemen."

With that, he motioned to the rear of the auditorium, where Stoddard was ushering in a troupe of white-jacketed barbers. Each one carried a folding chair and an electric clipper, which he plugged into the extension cord Stoddard had uncoiled along the back wall. Then the barbers turned on their clippers in unison, and the whole auditorium hummed like a beehive.

"I'm sure you'll give these hair stylists your complete cooperation," Hatfield smirked. "Good day, gentlemen."

So we all lined up like sheep to the shearing. There wasn't much to cut, since the dress code already specified that your hair couldn't cover your collar or ears. But that day we all got identical buzz cuts, with not much more than a five-o'clock shadow left on our scalps. If you didn't know better, you'd think it was the first day of Marine boot camp.

As we left the auditorium, Stoddard handed Chris and me our work assignment: the azalea detail. You see, the headmaster's wife was an azalea freak. Over the years she'd covered every corner of the campus with them. Naturally, she'd ordered a new batch of bushes flown in from Europe especially for the anniversary. Our job was to clear and plant a garden overlooking the football field. I forgot to mention that Donnel teams were called the Bears. Don't ask me why bears, rather than tigers or panthers. Maybe it's because they have such short tails. Anyway, in honor of the fiftieth anniversary, Hatfield had commissioned a bear statue to be installed in this garden and unveiled at the end of the day's festivities.

So we spent every afternoon that month manicuring the "bear patch" under old Mrs. Hatfield's critical gaze. I didn't really mind the gardening, but Chris was outraged.

[50]

Blairsville High School Library

"We should be practicing lay-ups, not rooting around in the dirt. What is this, a Siberian labor camp?"

Chris passed the afternoons plotting his revenge. First he wanted to chop down the trees in Hatfield's orchard. Then he decided that sabotaging his golf cart held more appeal. Each time he came up with a scheme, I'd put it down as being too risky or not imaginative enough. I wouldn't have minded getting back at Hatfield for those buzz cuts, but to tell the truth, I was afraid. If they found out who was behind those sorts of stunts, we'd surely get expelled.

But Chris was bent on action and eventually lost patience with my caution. "Whose side are you on?" he demanded one afternoon when I expressed doubts about the idea of stocking Hatfield's swimming pool with piranhas.

"I just don't want to get caught, is all."

"We can't pull off anything spectacular without taking risks," he argued. "But you're right about the piranhas—they're too crude. We've got to come up with something choice, something he'll remember till he croaks."

The statue arrived the day before the anniversary. We were spreading mulch over our just-completed garden when a truck pulled up alongside us. Three men unloaded a large marble pedestal and lugged it to the center of the garden while the sculptor looked on. Next came the statue, a life-sized bronze casting that must have weighed a ton. We watched the four of them wrestle it out of the truck.

"You boys over there," called the sculptor in a high-pitched voice. "Could you lend us the use of your strong young bodies?" He meant us.

We ambled over and each grabbed hold of a paw. Let me tell you, that was one heavy bear. We nearly busted a gut hoisting it onto the pedestal.

"Careful, careful!" piped the sculptor. "It's very delicate." Delicate my ass. "Turn it just a smidgen to the left . . . a titch more . . . perfect!"

We stepped back to have a look. It was a brown bear standing erect in a fighting stance, with fangs bared and taloned paws poised for combat.

"Well, what do you think, boys?" the sculptor asked.

"Must've cost Hatfield a pretty penny," responded Chris sourly.

The sculptor looked peeved at such a crass consideration. "If you want quality, you have to pay. The pedestal was cut from the best marble quarry in Portugal. And of course, *I* don't come cheap."

"It looks like a real bear," I offered.

The sculptor gazed lovingly at his creation. "I tried to capture his essential vulnerability."

That bear was about as vulnerable as a cobra. He looked ready to rip your throat out.

When he was done admiring his masterpiece, the sculptor wrapped it in a white sheet. Then he rigged a rope that could pull away the sheet with one simple tug. Chris watched him practice the unveiling with mounting interest.

"Of course—it's perfect!" he exclaimed in a hushed voice.

"What's your idea?"

"Forget it. You don't want to know."

"Sure I do." I wasn't sure.

"Nah. It's too risky for a Nervous Nelly like you."

He was taunting me, but I *was* nervous. "You'll need my help."

"Will I?" he asked defiantly. "This one's between me and Hatfield. I'll see you tomorrow."

And with that he was gone. I called him later that night to offer my assistance again. I guess I was more afraid of being left out than of getting caught. But Kitty answered the phone and told me Chris was staying overnight with a friend.

I caught up with him the next morning at the school assembly where Stoddard laid out the schedule for the day. Chris looked haggard, like he'd been up all night, but there was still a gleam in his eye. When I questioned him about his plan, he only smiled knowingly and assured me I'd find out soon enough. I knew it had something to do with the statue, but I couldn't figure out what. Maybe he'd dressed it up as a girl, or better yet, put an Afro wig and shades on it.

The anticipation was so intense I hardly got to enjoy the banquet. When they finally got ready to unveil the statue, I was the first one there to claim a ringside seat. Everyone crowded around—alumni, guests, and even a few newspaper photographers. Mrs. Hatfield took her place beside the sheet-draped statue, ready to pull the rope on cue. But her husband couldn't let this moment pass without a speech. He was having a ball—the king holding court at his coronation. While he went through his throat-clearing routine, Chris slipped into place beside me. If he was nervous, he didn't show it.

"This is a proud and happy moment for us all," began Hatfield, "and I'm pleased to share it with so many alumni and friends. For decades, Donnel has led the way in academic and athletic achievement. But more importantly, we have been the standard-bearer for values that some people seem to find outdated: integrity, loyalty, dedication. It is these qualities that our school mascot so nobly embodies. What more fitting symbol of tenacious courage could you find than the American brown bear? It is only fitting, then, that we commemorate our fiftieth anniversary with the installation of this statue. May it stand as a beacon of pride and inspiration for generations of Donnel Bears to come."

Chris led the applause as Mrs. Hatfield yanked the cord. But when the sheet fell aside, the crowd's clapping gave way to barely stifled giggles and gasps of dismay. The sculptor let out a shrill cry.

There on the marble pedestal stood a carnival-style teddy bear with a clutch of colorful helium balloons tied to its paw. The giggles gave way to belly laughs as the bear lifted gently off the pedestal and hovered whimsically in midair.

Hatfield went into conniptions. He sputtered something unintelligible and staggered forward, slashing his cane at the imposter. But as he lunged for it, the teddy bear levitated out of range, and Hatfield fell forward onto the pedestal. Stoddard ran to help him up, but Hatfield only beat him away with his cane. Brandishing it overhead, he turned and charged blindly into a pack of giggling schoolboys, who scattered like minnows before a shark.

Meanwhile, the teddy bear ascended blithely skyward, till it was only a colorful speck hanging high above the football field.

Chapter Nine

The heat was really on after that. Hatfield was determined to recover the statue and apprehend the culprits. He even offered a reward—two weeks' dismissal from study hall—to anyone giving information that led to the bear's recovery. Search parties were organized to scour the campus, but they all came up empty.

Chris was the prime suspect, but he didn't seem to mind. In fact he enjoyed the celebrity of it. He was confident he'd covered his tracks, and he knew they couldn't touch him without proof. I begged him to tell me where he'd hidden the statue, but he insisted I was better off not knowing.

He turned out to be right. A few days later Stoddard called us into his office for an "interview." At first he accused us outright, claiming one of the students had fingered us. When we played dumb, he threatened to expel us if we didn't confess.

"But sir," said Chris in his most angelic voice, "you know we'd help if we could. We're the ones who worked so hard on the garden, don't forget."

Stoddard wasn't buying. "I have my eye on you two.

Any more shenanigans around here and you're both history. Now get out of my office!"

Chris felt invulnerable, but it didn't rub off on me. I didn't care anymore where the bear was stashed, as long as no one ever found it. In the meantime, the fine marble pedestal stood sentinel in the garden like some huge conceptual sculpture: A Sugar Cube in Search of a Coffee Cup.

But the mystery of the missing bear soon faded from center stage as everyone's attention drifted toward Christmas vacation. Chris's family was going on a ski trip to Vermont, and I was invited along. I'd never skied before, but Chris promised to give me private lessons. My parents weren't thrilled with the idea—too expensive, too dangerous, too cold. But I had some money saved up from mowing lawns the past summer, and they finally agreed to rent me equipment as a Chanukah present.

Back at school, everyone was talking about the Christmas dance. I really wasn't interested, but it was hard not to feel left out. At the beginning of the term, all the first formers got engraved invitations to Miss Shippen's Dance Studio. Everyone but me and Bobby Meyers. You get the picture. Chris went a few weeks before dropping out and said I hadn't missed anything. But I still didn't know how to foxtrot.

And then there was the question of dates. Most of the guys were asking girls from Donnel's "sister school," Hilton Academy. And of course the only women at

Donnel were Mrs. Hatfield and the school nurse, who didn't count. There was a girl I knew from public school named Ellen Orlansky, but she had a serious acne problem, so I would have been embarrassed to show up with her.

Chris and I didn't discuss the situation until the week of the dance, when we were dressing in the locker room after basketball practice.

"You going to the dance?" I asked in an offhand sort of way.

"I dunno. Are you?"

"Nah. I don't think so."

Chris straightened his tie in the mirror. "I know a couple of girls we could invite."

"Yeah?" I tried not to sound too interested. "What do they look like?"

"They're okay. But why bother? We'd have to buy them corsages and gush all night about how great their dresses looked."

"Yeah," I agreed. "What's the point?"

"We could always go stag, y'know."

"You and me? Can we do that?"

"Sure. That way we'll be free agents."

I had a date for the dance.

It was billed as a black-tie affair, but Chris figured we could get away with wearing these two white dinner jackets that we found stashed in his attic. They were on the spacious side, but after we rolled up the sleeves and added a couple of red bow ties, we looked pretty sharp.

When we arrived on our bikes, everyone else was getting dropped off in front of the gym by their parents. I'd never been to a dance before, but this one looked more like a wedding. All the girls had on long dresses and white gloves, and the guys were mostly in tuxedos. There was even a receiving line at the door where you were supposed to introduce your date to the headmaster and his wife.

We were the only guys without dates, but that didn't seem to bother Chris. When we got to the head of the line, he took Mrs. Hatfield's gloved hand and pressed it to his lips.

"Charming dress you're wearing, Mrs. H. And such enchanting perfume," he crooned, sniffing at her wrist.

She giggled like a girl, but Mr. Hatfield wasn't amused. "Get your face away from my wife, Jordan! Where's your date?"

Chris felt around in his pockets, as if for a lost wallet, then looked searchingly to me. "Where're our dates? I thought you had 'em."

I blushed the color of my bow tie.

"I don't like clowns," growled Hatfield. He hooked the handle of his cane around Chris's neck and gave a firm yank. "Where's my statue, boy? Tell me or I'll rip your head off!"

"Paul—stop that this minute!" cried his wife, beating on his arm.

Hatfield released him with an angry snort, and Chris smiled tightly while he straightened his bow tie. "Merry Christmas, Scrooge," he muttered.

"Why don't you boys get some liquid refreshment," suggested Mrs. Hatfield.

"Good idea," I seconded, and dragged Chris away from the door.

The liquid refreshment was your basic Hawaiian Punch number with some sliced fruit floating on top. The gym was done over to look like an ocean liner, and the evening's theme—"Anchors Aweigh"—was scrawled on a banner stretched between the two basketball hoops. Perched on an elevated bandstand, the Mike Mosely Quartet played an up-tempo version of "Moon River" for the couples who glided across the floor. You'd never know it was the same court we'd been practicing fast breaks on that afternoon.

"What do we do now?" I asked, peering over the rim of my punch glass.

"Just troll for talent. Lots of fish in the sea."

We spotted McNair leading his date off the dance floor. She was this very mature-looking blonde named Donna Toomey who always showed up with him at football games. As soon as McNair went to get them punch, Chris moved in on her, guiding her back onto the basketball court for a slow dance. They were lost in the crowd by the time McNair returned. He looked so dumb standing there with those punch glasses, I couldn't help razzing him.

"Lost someone?"

"Er . . . no . . . she must've gone to the powder room," he murmured, looking for somewhere to put the glasses.

Chris and Donna waltzed back in our direction.

"They make a handsome couple, don't you think?" I said, pointing them out. McNair sighted them just as they melted back into the pack. All he could do was stand there and wait for the number to end.

"Where's his date?" he blustered.

"He doesn't have one. We came together."

"What are you guys, 'mos?"

"Why don't you ask Donna?"

The music had stopped, but they hadn't returned. McNair was craning his neck like crazy trying to spot them. Then we saw them leaving through the fire exit.

"Hold these," he said, brusquely handing me the glasses and spilling punch across my white jacket. He took off like a shot for the door. I got rid of the glasses and followed.

Chris already had her propped up against a dogwood tree out behind the gym. He was whispering something in her ear, and she was giggling her head off.

"Hey!" McNair shouted when the initial shock had worn off. "What's the big idea?"

Chris swatted his hand in McNair's direction, as if shooing away an insect. "Can't you see we want to be alone?"

Then he turned back to Donna, who was flustered and trying not to show it. McNair charged forward and grabbed Chris's shoulder. But instead of turning into McNair's roundhouse punch, Chris ducked under it. I never figured out where he got that sixth sense, but he sure seemed to need it a lot.

McNair's fist went flying into the tree trunk. You

could have heard him scream all the way across campus. Then Donna shifted into her Florence Nightingale routine, cooing and stroking his hand, which must have been busted in twenty places. Chris just shrugged and walked away.

He cracked up when he saw the raspberry stain on my jacket. "Who shot you?"

"The punch bowl. I can't go back in looking like this."

"Forget it. We'll have our own party."

He sauntered over to the Pepsi machine and bought two Mountain Dews. Then he directed me to the empty school buses lined up in the gravel lot behind the gym. He pulled open the door to the last bus.

"Your table is right this way, monsieur," he said with a deep bow. When we had reclined on the two rear benches, he drew a pint bottle of rum from his breast pocket, uncapping it with great ceremony.

"Puerto Rico's finest," he announced as he sniffed the bottle. "A delicate white rum with a surprisingly pungent boquet."

He took a swig and washed it down with a mouthful of Mountain Dew. "Ah . . . San Juan '68. A very good year."

He handed me the bottle and I took a sip.

"AAARGH!" It tasted like kerosene.

"Dew it—quick!"

He passed me the soda. I gulped it down, but the rum still burned in my throat.

"That's awful."

"It may taste bad, but it feels good after a few rounds."

"Where'd you get this?"

"From home. Now I'd like to toast the proud peoples of the Caribbean."

He took another swig and passed me the bottle. The second time around wasn't so bad. The burning sensation became a warm glow that reached to the back of my head.

By the time we had toasted Mrs. Hatfield's azaleas, the spirit of the Great Lost Bear, and each of Donna Toomey's round breasts, the bottle was empty.

"Donna Toomey," I sighed.

"Donna-toomey, donna-toomey, donna-toomey," Chris intoned.

It sounded like a tribal prayer, something you'd chant to make the rains come.

"I feel gr-r-reat!" I roared. And I did. I had never felt so great. "Sugar Frosted Flakes—they're gr-r-r-reat!

"Merry Christmas!" Chris toasted.

"I'd rather marry Donna Toomey. Let's go back in there and propose."

"Better not," he cautioned. "We're pretty drunk."

Somehow it hadn't occurred to me that I was drunk. Once, at a Passover seder, I drank four glasses of wine and fell asleep at the table. But this was different. I felt so light I thought I'd float away. But when I tried to get up off the seat, I ended up on the floor. It was the most comfortable floor I'd ever lain on.

"Drink, drank, drunk," I conjugated. Even my voice sounded great.

"Sink, sank, sunk," answered Chris from very far away.

He hauled me to my feet. *Who-o-o-sh!*

"Let's go for a walk," he commanded, steering me toward the front of the bus. It took us about ten minutes to get there because the bus was rocking back and forth so bad. It must have needed new shocks or something.

Chris sat me down in the driver's seat. "I'll be right back. Don't go away."

He must have been gone a while, because I fell asleep on the steering wheel. I was dreaming that Donna Toomey and I were dancing around a campfire when the horn woke me up.

"Pipe down in there!" It was Chris, sitting at the wheel of Hatfield's golf cart, smiling up at me through the windshield.

I stumbled out of the bus and the pavement leaped up to smack me in the face. As I climbed into the golf cart, I felt something warm and wet on my lips. No pain, just a tingling sensation and a salty taste. I touched my mouth and my finger came back red. Ordinarily I'm not too crazy about the sight of blood, especially my own. But that night it didn't bother me a bit. I just rubbed it off on my jacket. I thought it blended in nicely with the punch stain.

"Boy, are you a mess," said Chris.

"At least I'm not a thief. Where'd you find this, anyway?"

"It was parked out front."

"Hatfield will kill you if he—"

"Hold on tight!" he yelled as the cart lurched forward. Chris pushed the pedal to the floor and we took the first turn on two wheels, careening out of the parking lot.

"Where're we going?"

"To pick up Hatfield's Christmas present." Chris laughed.

I don't remember much about the ride except that we kept swerving off the path and almost flipped over a couple of times. Then we left the road and headed out across the playing fields. When the cart finally reeled to a halt, we were sitting in the middle of the azalea garden.

"I don't feel so good," I groaned. Actually I felt lousy, and the cart was spinning under me. I staggered out into the garden, which was spinning even worse.

"Don't fade out on me now, buddy," pleaded Chris. "We've got work to do."

I lay down in the azalea patch and passed out cold. When I came to, Chris was ripping up the bushes we'd spent so many hours planting.

"Stop!" I called out with as much force as I could muster. "What are you doing?"

He was digging with both hands, excavating a deep trench in the middle of the garden. He waved me over, and I crawled on all fours to peer into the hole. Staring up at me with bared fangs was the Great Lost Bear. I was so shocked to see him that I threw up on his face. I felt a little better after that.

"That's just great," muttered Chris. "Gimme your jacket."

"Not my jacket," I protested.

"What's the difference? It's already ruined."

He had a point there. I handed over the jacket, and Chris used it to wipe off the statue. "Now help me lift it out."

"Are you kidding? That thing weighs a ton."

"I got it in there alone. The two of us can get it out."

"What for?"

A slow smile spread across his face. He pointed down the hill to a manger scene, all strung with lights, that was set up in front of the gym.

"It's time for the Second Coming. Can't you see it? The Great Lost Bear cradled in the arms of the Blessed Virgin?"

All I could see was trouble. Since I had tossed my cookies, my head had cleared a bit. We had enough problems with a stolen cart on our hands. Moving the bear down the hill was strictly a kamikaze mission.

"There's no way to pull it off," I said.

"Sure there is. We load the bear into the cart, drive it down there, and lay it in the manger. Simple."

"But what if someone sees us?"

"We'll be in and out of there in a flash," he insisted. "No sweat."

I was sweating plenty, but there was no dissuading him. Together we managed to drag the statue out of the hole and hoist it headfirst into the cart. We were totally filthy by the time we finished, our faces caked with dirt and dried blood. We took one look at each other and broke out laughing. We laughed until our knees buckled. Then we slid to the ground and laughed some more.

All of a sudden Chris stopped laughing.

"Oh no—" he gasped. "Please, God—no . . ."

When I turned around to see what was happening, I thought I must still be drunk. The ground seemed to be moving under the cart. But it wasn't the ground. The golf cart—with the two bear legs protruding at a ludicrous angle—was rolling downhill!

Chris sprang to his feet and gave chase, but by this time the cart had picked up speed and was hurtling down toward the gym. With a flying leap, Chris grabbed hold of the bear's feet and hauled himself aboard. As I watched in speechless horror from the hilltop, I still half expected him to save the day—John Wayne reining in the runaway stagecoach. But John Wayne wasn't drunk when he did that stunt, and this wasn't the movies.

Chris had just scrambled into the driver's seat when the cart creamed into the manger. The three magi sailed through the air amid a blizzard of hay and a brilliant flash of shorted-out Christmas lights.

I stumbled down the hill to find Chris pinned on the ground beneath the mammoth bronze bear. He was beating against it wildly, hollering at the top of his lungs, "Get offa me, you big lunk!"

And then everyone was piling out of the gym to check out the commotion. The jig was up.

Chapter Ten

Chris got expelled right there in the wreckage of the manger as he lay helpless under a ton of bronze. I can still see Hatfield standing over him, waving his cane wildly in the air.

"You're out, Jordan! Out, out, OUT! I'll have you arrested!"

And he would have too, but when they lifted the statue off Chris, they found he'd broken his arm. So they called an ambulance instead of a squad car. I tried to go along with him to the hospital, but Stoddard dragged me into his office and called my parents to come pick me up.

That was the worst part. All the way home my mom kept repeating how "shocked and mortified" she felt, while my father conveyed his "deep disappointment." I was sick to my stomach and had to throw up twice before we got to the house.

The next day we had to have a special conference with Stoddard to decide my fate. I suffered through my first hangover while Stoddard expressed his hope that I would rehabilitate myself in the absence of "corrupting influences," meaning Chris. My parents, meanwhile, were falling all over themselves making excuses for me. I hated seeing them act like that. Finally, Stoddard decided to let me off with two weeks' suspension, but I wished he'd kicked me out too.

Needless to say, Christmas vacation was a bust. The ski trip was canceled, and Chris and I were both grounded. We weren't even allowed to talk on the phone. On Christmas Day my parents made a point of leaving me behind when they took my brother to a matinee of *2001: A Space Odyssey*. I didn't care. It gave me a chance to call Chris, who luckily answered the phone.

"How're you doing?"

"Just great," he whispered back. "I've got a twenty-pound cast on my arm and my father's threatening to send me to a military academy. Can you see me in some damn uniform, saluting teachers every time they pass?"

I couldn't picture it. "So what'll you do?"

"Sit tight, I guess, and hope the Christmas spirit smoothes things over."

"So, what'd you get for Christmas?" I asked, trying to lighten things up a little.

"A new pair of skis."

"Oh . . . swell . . ."

"Yeah."

A week later we were having dinner on New Year's Eve when the phone rang. I jumped up to answer it.

"If it's my partner," called my father from the dining room, "tell him I've gone out for the evening."

It was Chris.

"Can you talk?" he asked.

"Not really." My parents were only fifteen feet away.

"Then just listen. My father's enrolled me in Fallwell Academy."

"As in military academy?"

"That's right. And it's final. I'm supposed to leave the day after tomorrow for upstate New York." There was a pause. "I was hoping to see you before I go."

"Sure. When?"

"How about midnight, at the third tee?"

"Okay. I've gotta go now."

"Who was that?" my father asked when I returned to the table.

"Uh . . . Ellen Orlansky. She invited me to a New Year's Eve party."

"You're grounded."

"That's what I told her."

"Anyway, you're too young to go out on New Year's Eve," my mother chimed in for good measure.

It's true, I had never been out on New Year's Eve. Every year my father would fix an eggnog with a little rum for me and my brother to drink in front of the television set. Big deal. As usual, my parents were spending the night at the Kesslers' party. My mom got all dolled up, and my father made a big fuss about how sharp she looked. It was after eleven by the time they left.

"Don't wait up for us," my mother called gaily over her shoulder.

"And don't leave all the lights on," my father added.

As soon as they were gone, I looked in on my little brother. He was already asleep in bed, but I was supposed to wake him at quarter to twelve to watch the ball drop in Times Square. I knew he'd be pissed off if I let him sleep through it, so I set an alarm clock and left it by his bed along with a note:

Had to go out. Eggnog's in the fridge.
Happy New Year!

Then I rolled in the television set from my parents' room and turned it on without any sound. Guy Lombardo and his orchestra played silently in the Rainbow Room, while a boisterous crowd did a mime of drunken celebration. It seemed so unreal without the sound, as if they were all just pretending to have a good time. I looked over at my little brother, asleep in the TV glow, and tried to imagine him all grown up, dancing around drunk somewhere on some future New Year's Eve. Talk about depressing.

I grabbed my coat and scarf and ran out of the house. It was freezing cold, and the golf course was more than a mile away. That's where I was supposed to meet Chris, at the third tee of the Wildwood Country Club. It was the prettiest hole on the course, a par-five dogleg with a pair of kidney-shaped water traps guarding the green. There was a steep hill leading off the tee, where lots of kids liked to go sledding in the winter. But our spot was actually behind the tee. We'd discovered this huge old oak tree that was great for climbing. And it had a rotted-out trunk you could stand inside—that's how big it was.

My feet were frozen by the time I scaled the chain link fence into the golf course. A half foot of snow had fallen since Christmas, so the fairways were all silver in the moonlight. Only the old oak tree stood dark against the night sky.

I sprinted the last hundred yards and found Chris standing there in the shadow of the tree. The first thing I noticed was the cast, which stretched from the wrist to the shoulder on his left arm. It was weird to see him looking awkward and weighed down like that.

He waved his good hand weakly as I approached.

"Happy New Year," he said with a wan smile.

"Yeah, great. That's some load you're carrying."

He looked down at his cast and shook his head. "So much for the basketball season."

"Yeah, tough break." Bad joke.

Then a long silence.

"I just wish we could have pulled it off," he said finally.

"Yeah. We almost did."

"Yeah. . . ."

There was another awkward pause while I tried to think of something to say. "So . . . uh . . . you're heading north."

"Yeah. I thought about just taking off. Y'know, hitching down to Florida or somewhere. But my dad would have the cops after me in a flash, and they'd spot me easy with this thing on." He rapped the cast sharply with his good hand.

"They must have good skiing up north."

He shrugged. For a minute I thought he was about to break out crying, but he laughed instead. Then he took off his scarf.

"Gimme yours," he commanded.

I unwound mine—a plaid number my grandmother had given me for Chanukah—and handed it over. I thought he wanted to trade, but he tied them together as one and slung them around his neck. Then he vaulted up to the first branch, quick as a cat.

"Come on." He beckoned as he continued up the tree.

I was worried that he'd lose his grip and fall, but he did fine with his one good arm. In fact I had to work to keep up with him. I could hear him grunting with the effort, but he kept climbing higher and higher, till the branches started to creak and sway under his weight.

When I joined him up top, the wind was whistling through the branches, and the slender trunk seemed ready to snap off. It was scary and wonderful at the same time. You could see the whole golf course from up there and the houses and lawns beyond.

"Top o' the world!" he shouted above the wind.

You couldn't get much higher than that.

Then he crooked his cast around the trunk, and with his other hand he flung the scarves over the topmost branch.

"Gimme a hand," he said, and together we tied them fast. It was wicked cold up there, so we headed back down after a minute.

Once on the ground, we looked back up at the scarves, flying like a defiant banner at an impossible height.

"That's great," he laughed. "Everyone will wonder how the hell they got there, and who did it. But we'll know, won't we?"

"Yeah. And someday maybe we'll come back and get them."

"Definitely. We'll definitely do that."

We lapsed into silence. I was suddenly freezing cold.

"I'm not much of a letter writer," he said.

"Me neither."

"Well, I'll be back. Till then you keep 'em guessing, okay?"

"Okay. You too."

He nodded his head slowly, like he was trying to remember something. Then he sort of punched my shoulder with his good hand. I wanted to grab hold of him and hang on, but he turned and ran away down the hill.

I backed up and leaned into the hollow of the tree. For a minute I thought I could hear the sap running through the trunk. But then I realized it was just the blood racing through my head.

So I just stood there shivering and watching as his shadowed figure receded into the field of silver snow.

Part Two

Have you ever been
Have you ever been to Electric Ladyland?
The magic carpet waits for you
So don't you be late.

—Jimi Hendrix

Chapter Eleven

When my train pulled into Union Station, my father was waiting on the platform to meet it. He didn't hug me or anything, but he carried my bag to the car, which was parked illegally out front. You can do that if you're a doc—leave your car parked just about anywhere with a "Doctor On Call" sign propped up inside the windshield. Ordinarily my father doesn't like to, but I guess this was a special case.

We drove quietly through downtown with the windows rolled up tight because of the cold—past the Capitol building, past the White House. My father asked some questions about my finals, but I didn't answer, so after a while he quit trying. He said he was going on rounds at University Hospital and I could look in on Chris there if I wanted to. The way he said "look in on" instead of "visit" should have tipped me off.

I never did like hospitals—I guess no one does—but I've spent a fair amount of time in them with my father. When I was a kid and he took me to ball games, he'd usually have to stop off on the way to the stadium to see some patients. I'd pad along behind as he strode down the corridors talking to nurses and interns, checking charts and giving orders, ducking in and out of patients' rooms. He didn't actually introduce me to anyone, but they all knew that the kid wearing the Senators cap or carrying the Redskins pennant was the doctor's son. Sometimes a nurse or a patient would smile at me, but it just made me nervous, like I was supposed to do something for them. And the hospital smells—the disinfectant odor mixed with disease—gave me a nauseous feeling that wouldn't go away till the third inning.

So there we were again, walking down the corridor with me trailing behind like always. My father was whistling softly through his teeth in this officious manner he has in hospitals, but I was sort of in a daze and almost forgot what I was doing there—till we came up on the swinging double doors marked *INTENSIVE CARE: Authorized Entry Only*.

The first thing that hits you when walk into an intensive care unit is the noise. It's not the usual hospital noise of TV sets and patients complaining to nurses about the lousy food. The patients aren't making a peep, but still, there's a regular racket. Each patient is hooked up to about five different machines, and every one of those contraptions has its own beeping or clicking or wheezing sound. It's like you're in a goddamn factory.

There weren't any private rooms in the ward, just two long rows of beds, so the nurse had to point us toward Chris. He was at the far end of the ward, and his father was sitting stone still at the foot of his bed watching the vital-sign monitors beep up and down. I was sure glad not to find Kitty there. It's not the sort of place a mother should have to be.

Mr. Jordan shook hands with my father and nodded curtly to me. After my father flipped through the clipboard charts that hung at the foot of the bed, he led Mr. Jordan out to the hall for a talk, while I stayed there with Chris. When I finally got up the nerve to look, I barely recognized him. The top of his head was covered with bandages, and his eyes were swollen shut. A respirator fit snugly over his nose and mouth, and there were all sorts of tubes running in and out of his arms. The pulse and temperature sensors pasted to his chest were connected by wires to a group of monitors alongside the bed. It was hard to tell where Chris ended and the hardware began.

His right hand was lying by his side, so I picked it up and squeezed. He didn't squeeze back, but at least his hand was warm. It was no use talking to him, so I pressed his hand to my forehead and tried to signal him that I was there and it was okay to wake up now. But he didn't wake up or rustle the sheets or anything. And those machines kept on doing their damn beeping clicking buzzing thing.

Looking down there at him, all hooked up and so helpless he could barely breathe without some machine showing him how, I tried to remember the way he looked running or jumping—or even just laughing. He used to laugh at all the things that scared me most. A truly fearless laugh—unafraid of headmaster or girls or falling out of trees and getting hurt. Right then I wondered if he was even afraid of dying, or just laughing silently to himself about it.

Then suddenly it hit me. Chris wasn't there in that bed, wasn't connected to that hand I held in mine. He was already dead, and those machines were just keeping his body warm with blood and breath and sugar water. He was gone.

He was gone, and there was nothing my father or any of these fancy machines could do to change that. He was only being kept alive because no one could bear to turn off the machines and let a nineteen-year-old boy stop breathing—even though his brain had forgotten how, had been bounced too hard in ways a brain shouldn't be. And there was nothing to be done about it.

He was gone. But where exactly had I lost him? On that snowy New Year's Eve? Could I have somehow held him there, safe inside the tree with me forever? Were there other moments—later on—times when I might have reached out and pulled him back from the edge?

I dropped his hand to the bed and turned toward the door. It was all I could do to keep from breaking into a run, for even as I walked away from him, I could feel his eyes on my back, and deep inside my head I could hear his laughter calling after me like an echoing dream.

Chapter Twelve

I didn't see Chris the whole time he was away at military school. You wouldn't think you could lose touch with a best friend like that, but it happens. We wrote a couple of letters and even spoke on the phone once, but it wasn't the same. It wasn't like we could make plans together or joke about stuff anymore. So after a few months we let it drop. After that he never seemed to come home for vacations, even in the summer. I figured he was still sore at his father for shipping him off to a military academy.

I stuck it out at Donnel for a couple of more years, but I didn't make close friends after he left. I really didn't want another buddy, and I wasn't about to confirm Stoddard's theory—that crack he made about me being better off without Chris. I wasn't better off. I was lonely a lot, and I couldn't see the point of playing football anymore. But I learned how to keep myself company again, the way I had to before Chris came along.

I got by okay, except for the girl problem. The problem, of course, was that there weren't any around. Somewhere out there a sexual revolution was under way—it even made the cover of *Life* magazine. But the ramparts were so far from the walls of Donnel School, it wasn't funny. In fact it was downright abnormal, and you didn't have to be a genius to figure that out. Even my parents could, and me turning out *ab*normal was their worst nightmare. So they finally caved in and let me go back to public school after the third form.

Catching up on the girl situation was my main mission in tenth grade. And believe me, I had a lot of ground to cover. For starters, I'd missed out on sex education, which public school kids got in the eighth and ninth grades. At Donnel, biology class never ventured below the waist. Nervous system, respiratory, circulatory—that was it. Even the digestive system was deemed too close to home. But that wasn't the real obstacle. Hell, my dad was a doctor, so I figured he could always fill me in on the technical details. The problem was that I'd been out of action for three years. I'd barely spoken to a girl since sixth grade, much less tried to put the make on one. Women can get to seem pretty strange when you've been away from them that long.

It reminded me of this old Henry Fonda movie where he plays a very rich guy who's been "up the Amazon" for a couple of years trapping snakes for some museum. When he finally makes it back to civilization, there're all these gold-digging dames waiting to snare him. Only he's been in the jungle so long, he doesn't know which end is up with women anymore. It's really a scream. Anyway, that's how I felt when I made it back to public school, like I'd been up the Amazon for three years. Except I wasn't rich and I didn't look like a movie star, so the girls weren't exactly lining up for me.

The only thing I had going for me was poetry. You see, my second-form English teacher, Mr. Dickson, was a poetry freak. That's all we read from September to June, and he made us memorize a poem every week. It was sort of a drag at the time, but I have to admit it came in handy. You see, it turns out that women go crazy over the stuff. Don't ask me why, but believe me, it's the one thing I ever figured out about them. It doesn't have to be a love poem. It doesn't even have to rhyme, for chrissakes. But as soon as they hear you spouting something in verse, you're golden. I swear to god. It's sort of like giving flowers, which by the way is another corny routine that almost never fails.

Say you're after some really gorgeous girl and you want to tell her how beautiful she is. Well, she knows that, and she's heard it from every creep on the make since she was twelve years old. But you toss her a few lines of Byron, something about

> . . . *that nameless grace*
> *Which waves in every raven tress*
> *Or softly lightens o'er her face*

and you'll have her eating out of your hand. It even works the other way around. Say you want to drop your girlfriend, but you don't know how to break it to her. If you can come up with something like

> *You must remain, I must depart;*
> *Two autumns falling in the heart.*

she'll think you're a sensitive, tortured soul, instead of a no-good heel. She may even feel sorry for you.

Now I realize it's hard to deliver lines like that with a straight face. No sweat. Just scribble it down and pass it to her in class, or slip it into her locker. That way she can moon over it all night. But if you write it down, you're better off adding the real poet's name, just in case she's read it before. You still get points for knowing that her "nameless grace" is beyond mortal words.

Tenth grade was also the year I found out about movies. Now I know this sounds old-fashioned, but nothing beats hanging out with a girl at an afternoon movie. Especially in one of those "art" theaters that just shows old flics from the thirties and forties. Let's face it, *2001: A Space Odyssey* is *not* a sexy movie. But take a picture like *Casablanca*. At first glance you'd think it's about patriotism and honor. But it's really all about sex. Believe me, I've seen it a dozen times. Same with *Gone With the Wind*. Sure there's a Civil War going on, and yeah the Yankees are burning down Atlanta, but all Rhett Butler can think about is getting into Scarlett O'Hara's pants. Talk about your timeless themes.

Also, those kinds of theaters are almost empty in the afternoon, and you'd be surprised what a girl will do in an empty theater. Or maybe you wouldn't, but I sure was. Now don't get the wrong idea. I wasn't making out like a bandit or anything. Just getting down the fundamentals—sort of like spring training. To tell the truth, I struck out most of the time, and if it hadn't been for Lord Byron and Clark Gable, I'd never have gotten to first base. They were my only coaches—till Chris showed up.

It was the last day of classes, and everyone was lounging around on the lawn in front of school saying goodbye before summer vacation. I was sitting next to Brenda Bucknell, trying to lure her to a matinee of *Mutiny on the Bounty*—the '35 version with Gable and Laughton and a thousand Polynesian girls. Brenda was stretched out in front of me on the lawn, doodling little flowers on the back of her hand with a ballpoint pen. She was also fond of dotting her i's with circles and writing o's in the shape of hearts.

"You don't want to miss the original," I urged, marveling at how she stroked the grass with her bare foot. "It's much better than the remake."

"But it's such a scrumptious day," she cooed. "It would be a crime to sit in a dark theater all afternoon."

Sitting wasn't exactly the crime I had in mind. Brenda had this amazing mane of long blond hair that bounced against her ass when she walked. It was really something to see. So what if she used words like "scrumptious" and "marv"? Nobody's perfect.

I plucked a dandelion and tossed it into her hair.

"Do-on't! I just washed it."

I was getting nowhere fast.

Then she started telling me about her summer job as a camp counselor, and how she had a crush on this really cute arts-and-crafts instructor. She showed me the lanyard he'd made for her out of orange and black gimp, which were his school colors. Here I was offering this girl a unique cinematic experience, and she talks to me about lanyards!

I was about to try another dandelion when I spotted him. What caught my eye, actually, was his bicycle—a shiny ten-speed racer, its spokes ablaze with sunlight—weaving lazy figure eights through the pockets of sunbathing girls on the lawn. Something about its slow-motion grace tipped me off, the way it dipped and turned like a hawk circling its prey. His back was to me, and I was afraid to call out his name, afraid he was just some wishful mirage. But then he swerved toward me, and there was no mistaking his smile. In an instant he was dismounting in front of me. The cavalry had arrived.

He was a few inches taller, but otherwise he looked about the same. His hair was cropped short in a severe military cut, which, along with his stiff new jeans, made him stand out from the other kids. At that time the dress codes in public schools had collapsed and everyone was racing to see how long they could grow their hair, how faded they could get their jeans.

"Private Jordan, reporting for duty, *sir!*" He snapped a smart salute.

I returned the salute. "At ease, Private. What are you doing out of uniform?"

"I got time off for bad behavior." He winked.

"How much time?"

"Forever. They kicked me out!"

"Yeah? What'd you do?"

"Everything I could think of." He smiled down at Brenda. "Hello."

"Hi." She smiled back. "You must be a friend of . . . uh . . ."

"Danny," I had to prompt. Jesus.

Chris dropped noiselessly to the ground. "I'm Chris. And you are . . . ?"

"Brenda."

"Delighted to meet you." Chris reached out and shook her bare foot, then rotated it slowly and studied the sole with great seriousness. She giggled. "I see a tall dark stranger in your future. Eight feet tall and very strange." More giggles.

Then he dropped her foot and turned back to me. "So, what're you doing today?" he asked, as if he'd only left a week ago.

"I don't know. I was thinking about a movie."

"Forget it. Let's take a ride."

"But I didn't bring my wheels."

"No problem." He leaped aboard his bike and motioned to the seat. Ordinarily I'd have felt funny riding on the back of a guy's bike, but I climbed right on.

"Have a good summer," I called to Brenda.

"Are you going here next fall?" She was talking to Chris, of course.

He shrugged. "That's a long time from now. I've got to make it through the summer first." With a laugh he pushed off, and we went sailing down the path away from school.

The circus was back in town, and I had the best seat in the house.

Chapter Thirteen

Chris waved a salute to the uniformed guard as we whooshed through the stone gatehouse of Wildwood Country Club. We fairly flew around the tennis courts and past the practice putting greens, picking up speed as we glided onto the asphalt path leading to the first tee.

"Road hogs!" called Chris as we zipped past a fleet of electric golf carts.

"So why'd they kick you out?" I shouted over the rushing wind.

"Said I was destructive to company morale." He steered off the path and headed across the fairway. " 'Conduct unbecoming to an officer and a gentleman.' "

"Meaning . . . ?"

We had reached the second tee, where two old men were preparing to drive. "Meaning I like to get high. Fore!" called Chris as he swerved in front of them and pointed the bike straight downhill. I had to grab his waist to keep from falling as we careened downward, the bike gathering speed.

"M-A-R-I-J-U-A-N-AAA!!!!" he hollered at the top of his voice as the bike plummeted toward the water trap at the base of the hill. At the last minute he cut sharply, skidding the rear wheel around. The bike stopped dead, teetered, and fell over sideways into the rough.

"Handles like a song, don't she?" He smiled.

As we disentangled ourselves from the handlebars, a golf ball shot past our heads.

"Better find some cover," I said.

Another ball whizzed by and we dove under a willow tree back in the deep rough.

"So . . . uh . . . you smoke pot?" I asked. I don't know why it surprised me. Maybe it was the idea of drugs at a military academy.

"Sure. Don't you?"

"Well . . . once in a while," I stammered. "Y'know, sometimes."

I'd actually smoked once, at the cast party for a play I'd acted in earlier that year. It was a bit part—my character didn't even have a name, just THE SECOND POLICEMAN—but I got invited to the party along with the rest of the cast, which was mostly upperclassmen. About halfway through the party, this senior girl who'd played THE MAID came up and whispered in my ear, "You wanna turn on?" I didn't know what she meant, so I just nodded my head as she hooked her arm through mine and led me toward the rear bedroom. I thought maybe she liked younger guys, but that wasn't it.

The room was dark except for a few candles stuck in wine jugs. About twenty kids were sprawled out on the carpeted floor, smoking a water pipe. THE MAID cleared us a space by the pipe and showed me how to smoke it. I spent the rest of the party sucking furiously on that thing, but for some reason I couldn't get stoned. Everyone else seemed to be having a great time, so I didn't say anything. But I felt like I'd blown it.

That was the sum total of my experience with pot.

Chris pulled a plastic bag of grass from his hip pocket and began rolling a joint in his lap. The idea of smoking pot in the middle of a golf course seemed pretty risky. I could see half a dozen golfers from where we sat, but Chris didn't seem to care. I couldn't help noticing how easily he handled the pot, like it was just tobacco.

"So what're you up to this summer?" I asked.

"Fighting with my old man mostly. I've only been back a week and he's already on my case."

"What about?"

"Well, he wasn't exactly thrilled to death about my dishonorable discharge. On top of which they booted me right before exams, which means I have to make up my science credit over the summer."

"Summer school?"

"*And* he expects me to find a job. Otherwise he's threatening me with another academy. I guess you could say I'm on probation."

"Well, I've got to find a job too."

"Yeah? Maybe we could do something together."

"Great, but it's hard enough finding one job, much less two."

"We could always caddy," he said, sealing the joint with an expert spin of the thumbs. "I know the pro."

"You mean here?"

"Sure. He used to give me lessons."

"Sounds good to me."

"Solid."

He lit the joint and inhaled, smiling broadly as the smoke filled his lungs. When he passed it to me, I took a test drag on it, then a bigger one.

"Hold it in your lungs as long as you can," he coached.

We passed the joint back and forth, taking in as much smoke as we could without coughing it up. I could tell by his marbleized eyes that Chris was already stoned, but I didn't feel a thing. Somehow, I knew I never would. That was my fate—to go through life watching other people get high. There was something wrong with my brain cells. It was so sad, I wanted to cry. I thought I would too, but I started to laugh instead. It began in my stomach as a giggle, gathered speed as it rolled up my chest, and finally crashed through my head like a ten-pin strike. And all of a sudden our three-and-a-half-year separation collapsed in on itself—*ppffft!*—and there we were, laughing together in the deep rough off the third fairway on the first day of summer vacation. And there was no doubt about it—I was stoned!

"Hey, I'm hungry. What about you?" I heard someone ask. Must have been Chris. There was no one else around.

Come to think of it, I *was* hungry, so I said so. "I've never been so hungry."

"I know where to find a pretty fair cheeseburger," he announced.

"Let's go!" I shouted, on my feet at once and ready to run to the moon.

We raced to the clubhouse instead. The front patio was filled with golfers who sat at tables under brightly colored umbrellas sipping gin and tonics. Everyone was holding a putter, which seemed pretty funny to me, but when I started to giggle, Chris gave me a sharp elbow to the ribs. So I sat down at a table and scanned the short-order menu. The words were floating across the page like Scrabble pieces.

"You order," I said, folding the menu in my lap. When a skinny waitress with braces came toward us, the giggles started up again, so I retreated behind the menu.

"Look who's back from the wars," she said, smiling at Chris.

"A.W.O.L.'s more like it."

"What's the matter? Didn't like taking orders?"

"I'll leave that to you. We'll have four bacon cheeseburgers, two Cokes, and fries."

"You expecting company?"

"No, just the two of us—and we're hungry."

"That's one word for it." She smirked. "What's with your friend?"

I didn't budge from behind my screen.

"Oh, Danny's a little bashful is all. Great guy though, once you get to know him. Danny, say hello to Becky."

But when I peered out from behind the menu, she had vanished. I was feeling a little paranoid by this time. "Everyone seems to be staring at us," I thought I'd mention to Chris.

"Relax," he said. "Most of the people here are as

bombed as we are. That's the whole point of hanging out at a country club."

"Yeah, but they look so weird. Why are they all wearing white shoes?"

"So you can see them in the dark."

That cracked us up.

"What's so funny?" It was Becky, back already with a tray full of food.

She was. We were both giggling now.

"Uh . . . can we get these to go?" asked Chris.

Becky cocked her head sideways. "You want me to wrap them up?"

"No thanks, we'll just take them with us."

Chris signed the check and gathered the cheeseburgers into his arms. I followed his lead, balancing the fries on my menu and wedging a soda into the crook of each arm. Becky seemed to want her menu back, but I couldn't bear to leave it behind. It was my shield. I knew I'd be all right, though, as soon as we got off that patio. . . .

"Christopher Jordan—well I'll be damned!" someone shouted.

"Oh, shit," Chris groaned under his breath. "Just let me do the talking."

He had nothing to worry about on that score. No way I was talking to anyone. A boyish-looking character with a middle-aged paunch advanced on us, his hand outstretched in greeting. At first I thought he had bright-green legs, but then I realized they were just his pants.

"You made general yet, you old dog?" he cried out heartily.

"No sir, not yet," said Chris as he loaded the burgers onto my menu and shook hands with Mr. Green Jeans.

"You guys going on a picnic, or what?"

"Oh, no sir. Actually, we were looking for you," said Chris, smiling broadly now. "Danny, this is Sammy Howe, the club pro I was telling you about."

He stuck out a hand, but I couldn't get mine free without upsetting my load. He let it pass.

"As a matter of fact," Chris continued, "we were hoping to do some caddying for you."

"Well now, Christopher, you know how I feel about hiring club members. I'd much rather see you out there on the practice tee, getting in shape for the Juniors Tournament. You used to have a dandy touch with the irons."

"I haven't really played much since I broke my arm. But caddying would at least give me a chance to get back on the course."

Sammy looked us over, finally nodding his assent. "All right. You're on. You guys report to the caddy master tomorrow at eight o'clock sharp." And with a wave, he was gone.

So we had our summer jobs. Just that simple, just that quick.

"Stick with me, buddy," said Chris as he tossed down a burger in a single gulp. "We're gonna have a blast."

The burgers were in serious disarray, so I grabbed a handful of fries. I could tell this was going to be some kind of summer. And it was only three hours old.

Chapter Fourteen

That night at dinner I was proud to announce that I'd already lined up a summer job. My parents were pleased, till they got the details. It turned out that Chris was still on their no-goodnik list. Didn't they have enough bad influences to worry about, what with my hair growing over my collar and my knees poking out through my jeans?

"But Chris has a crew cut and brand-new jeans," I argued in his defense.

"He probably got kicked out of school again, the *gonif*," my mother grumbled as she delivered the roast to the table.

"Which way do I slice this, honey?" asked my father, probing the meat with the carving knife.

"Oh, Sol, just find the grain and cut across it. You're the surgeon, remember?"

"What's a *gonif*?" my brother Mark wanted to know.

"A thief," my mother said. "Why can't you wash your hands *before* you come to the—"

"Are you calling Chris a thief?" I was outraged.

"He stole that statue, didn't he?" My father came to her rescue, like always.

"No, he didn't steal it. He hid it. And I don't like you talking about my friend like that."

"Wonderful friends you choose."

"What I don't understand," said my mother, "is why you have to spend your summer carrying bags for a bunch of anti-Semites."

"Who are you calling anti-Semites?"

"It's a well-documented fact"—my father's turn now—"that Wildwood Country Club doesn't encourage Jewish membership. Couldn't you find a job that uses your mind a little?"

"Well I'm sorry, but the Mayo Clinic wasn't hiring tenth graders this summer."

"Don't get sarcastic with your father, young man." My mom hates sarcasm.

"It's a job, okay? You wanted me to get a job, so I got one."

"Wonderful job. My son the beast of burden."

And on and on till I finally leaped up from the table and charged out of the room while my father hollered after me that running away doesn't solve anything.

I went up to my room, lay back in bed, and clamped on my headphones. I put on Jimi Hendrix's latest album. It seemed like a long time since I first heard him sing that day in Chris's basement. In the meantime, the promise of the *Life* magazine cover had finally come true. The tightly clenched world of Donnel School had opened up like a ripe flower—and Chris was here to celebrate with me. The timing of our reunion seemed almost cosmic, as if our friendship had been suspended till all the heavenly bodies were properly aligned, till the world was turned upside down and inside out—and everyone was dancing in the aisles to rock 'n' roll music. It was like *The Time Tunnel* when the guys always arrive on the scene at the splashiest moments of history. Like magic. But I couldn't expect my parents to understand that.

I met Chris outside the country club at eight o'clock sharp the next morning. The caddy master gave us each a cap with a WCC insignia.

"Now you be sure to keep that hair up under your cap," he said to me. "This is a refined club."

So we sat around the caddy shack, which is sort of like a baseball dugout, waiting for the caddy master to send us out. At noon we were still waiting. The only caddy left besides Chris and me was this old guy named Willie, who looked like he'd been hauling bags all his life.

"Folks nowadays seem to like them electric carts," he complained to us. "Now wouldn't you think they'd get enough of driving during the week, be ready for a little exercise on Saturday morning? And can you show me a cart that'll read a green or hold a flag? No sir, I bet you can't."

The caddy master stuck his head in the shack. "Willie, I'm sending you out with a foursome to show these boys the ropes."

Our foursome was two middle-aged couples, and you could tell just by looking at them that they were duffers.

"Shee-eet," groaned Willie under his breath. "First he parks my ass in the shack all morning, and then he hands me these turkeys."

He quickly hoisted the two men's bags onto his shoulders. They were the bigger ones, and I thought he was doing us a favor, leaving us to split the women's. But he was no dope. At least the men could hit straight.

Our bags weren't very heavy, at least not at first. But it was the hottest part of the day and the women couldn't keep their balls on the course. Chris and I were zig-zagging our way up and down the fairways, in and out of the woods, and all the time listening to them yak back and forth to each other. I swear to god they were more interested in talking than playing golf. By the time we reached the seventh tee we were really hurting.

"Let's see now. What club do I use on this hole, Barb? I can never remember," said Sue, the one I was caddying.

"You always use a three wood, but I think you'd do better with a five," coached Barb as she teed up.

"Hmm . . . let me see the five wood, caddy."

Each of her woods had a little hand-knit cap with a number stitched on it. I bared the five wood for her inspection.

"No, I think I'll go with the three. Never mix, never worry."

She hooked her tee shot over the trees into the adjoining fairway.

"Fore!" Barb called out. "You're supposed to yell 'Fore!' when you do that." Barb swung, and shanked her ball into the woods. "FORE!"

Chris groaned miserably.

"You forgot to keep your head down," Sue chided. "I saw you look up."

After rooting around in the woods for five minutes, Chris emerged with Barb's ball. She took a drop and sliced her next shot into the water trap guarding the green. Chris's head drooped to his chest.

"Oh dear. That was my lucky ball," Barb clucked.

"Looks like a bad-luck ball to me," said Chris under his breath.

"You don't understand. I once shot a hole-in-one with that ball. It has tremendous sentimental value to me. You simply must retrieve it."

Chris circled the water hole, peering into the murky water.

"I can see it," he announced when he finally spotted the ball, "but it's about ten feet in. Sorry."

"I don't think I can play without that ball."

"I got news for you, lady. You can't play *with* it."

"Is that your job, to insult the club members? I want that ball back," she insisted.

"Then help yourself, lady. No way I'm ruining my sneakers for a fucking golf ball."

Then her husband got into it. "I'll thank you to watch your language around my wife. Now go get that ball, or I'll report you to the caddy master."

Chris stared hard at the guy, then looked away toward the horizon, trying to steady his temper. I followed his gaze to the big old oak by the third tee. Sure enough, our scarves were still flying, though somewhat battered by the elements. A slow smile spread across his face as Chris unslung the golf bag from his shoulder and hefted it in his hands.

"Whoa, boy," murmured Willie behind me.

I was about to offer to go after the ball myself when the bag entered the water with a colossal splash and sank quickly out of sight. Barb only watched in shocked silence, but her husband sputtered a curse and hurled his putter at Chris, who was already cantering away down the fairway.

I dropped my bag and followed after him.

Blairsville High School Library.

Chapter Fifteen

I had to run to catch up to him a block away from the club. He finally slowed down to a walk when I pulled abreast of him.

"Way to go," I said, shaking my head. "Always the big gesture."

"That job was all wrong for us."

"Maybe. But at least it was a job."

"You expect me to stick around and take that kind of crap?"

"I don't expect you to pull a stunt like that our first day on the job."

"You want to spend your summer playing mule to those clowns? Go ahead, I'm not stopping you."

"I thought the idea was to work together. You could have at least asked me before tossing away our jobs like that."

"Hey, listen . . . I'm sorry, really. But what could I do?" A grin lit across his face. "Did you see her expression when I gave her bag the heave?"

I was still pissed off, but I had to fight back a smile at the memory of those sinking clubs.

"And him? What about that guy?" He nudged me playfully.

"You know you came about three inches away from getting a putter through the skull."

"Nah. He didn't have the arm for it."

I had to laugh at that, but I didn't want to let him off that easy. "So what are we gonna do all summer, wise guy? I sure hope you have something cooking on the back burner."

"As a matter of fact, I've been giving that some thought."

"Ten whole minutes' worth?"

"Ever since the first tee, actually. And when I caught sight of our scarves up there, I knew I was right. We're idiots to work as pack animals for rich jerks like that. We should be doing something to stretch our brains."

"Hah. That's what my folks said."

"They're right."

"So what did you have in mind?"

"Chemistry."

"Chemistry?"

"Chemistry 103, with Miss Jenkins. I hear she's a fox."

"Isn't she the one who wears that creepy green eye shadow?"

"C'mon. It'll be fun. We can be lab partners."

"Sounds like a real blast. My summer in chemistry class."

"Just think about it, okay? It sure beats working."

"Except we still have to get jobs."

"Who'll have time for a job?" He winked. "The

serious study of chemistry is a very demanding pursuit." He pointed across the street at a McDonald's. "Hey, look at those golden arches. Don't they just make your mouth water?"

But it turned out that burgers weren't all Chris had in mind. He'd arranged to buy some grass from a senior named Dewy whom I knew vaguely as the drummer in a local rock band. Dewy hadn't shown yet, so we decided to have a bite.

I'd never scored drugs before, but the parking lot across from the neighborhood McDonald's seemed out of line. I mean, there were women and children eating in there, not to mention undercover narcs probably lying in wait behind the tall golden trash cans.

"By the way," said Chris between mouthfuls of Big Mac, "Dewy says he's got some dynamite acid. Maybe we should buy a few hits as long as we're at it."

LSD-25: d-lysergic acid diethylamide, better known as acid. Even the name gave me the creeps. Sounded like something that ate away your brain in layers. Sure, there were plenty of groovy rock ballads about the stuff, but I'd also heard the stories of people freaking out on bad trips, thinking they were birds and flying out of windows. Of course, those were the articles my mom had clipped from the papers and left on my dresser next to the freshly folded laundry.

"I don't know about that stuff," I said. "Some weird Swiss chemist makes an accidental discovery, and I'm supposed to eat it?"

"All the biggest scientific discoveries are accidental,"

Chris argued. "What about penicillin?"

"Penicillin doesn't make you hallucinate and think you're Jesus Christ."

Chris took a different tack. "There are no true accidents—there's only destiny. LSD was destined to be discovered, and we were destined to live in that era. Why question fate?"

"And you were destined to heave that golf bag into the drink, right?"

"Just thought I'd mention it." He shrugged.

About two hours and four cheeseburgers later Dewy's hand-painted van rolled into the parking lot.

"Let's go," said Chris, getting to his feet.

I tried stalling. "But I, uh . . . I haven't finished my drink."

"Toss it," he said, and sauntered out to the van.

Chris tapped twice on the rear window, and Dewy's bloodshot eyes appeared behind the parted curtain. The door to the back of the van slid open and we scurried inside. The door slammed shut behind us.

"How you dudes doin'?" said Dewy. "I'll be right with ya."

We weren't his only customers that afternoon. A slinky blond girl with green granny glasses was sitting cross-legged in front of a plate piled high with tiny, bright-orange tablets. She was counting them out into mounds of fifty while Dewy's eyes danced from pile to pile, tailing her every move. Rumor had it that Dewy was a speed freak, but I thought he might just be a high-energy type of guy.

The seats had been cleared from the back of the van, but the deep pile carpet was soft to sit on. We were huddled in a tight circle around the plate, and I'd landed right next to the girl so that our knees were actually touching. Chris sat across from me with his eyes trained on the transaction.

"You sure these are four-way barrels?" asked the girl in a low husky voice.

"Straight from my man on the coast. Satisfaction guaranteed."

"This the Orange Sunshine you were telling me about?" Chris asked.

"The same. Forty a hundred, three hundred a thou. You in the market for some?"

Chris gazed wistfully at the anthills of orange microdots, then raised his eyes to mine. It was hard to believe something so small could do any harm. Then again, I wasn't eager to test that theory.

"We'll take a rain check on those, thanks," I said firmly. "What about the weed?"

"Got it right here," said Dewy. "Take a taste."

Dewy dragged a large plastic garbage bag full of grass from under the front seat. Chris opened the top and stuck his face inside, then motioned to me to do the same. It smelled like a florist shop.

"Top-o'-the-line Colombian," said Dewy, handing me a pack of cigarette papers. "Roll yourself a doobie. Stay awhile."

Well, I was pretty sure what he meant by a doobie, but I had no idea how to roll one. Luckily, everyone's attention was fixed on the acid count while I fumbled around with the grass. My doobie ended up looking like it had swallowed something fat and round. I tossed it back into the bag and passed the papers to Chris, who rolled a perfect joint without even looking.

I fired it up and passed it to the girl. She was busy loading the acid into a mason jar and motioned to me to hold the joint up to her lips. As I watched her inhale from my hand, I realized she was a lot older than us. Not even in high school, probably. Then she winked at me over her sunglasses, which made me look away.

"I count a thousand, even," she announced as she pulled out a tremendous wad of money and peeled off six fifties. "I hope they're as trippy as you say."

"First-class tickets or your money back." Dewy smiled and stuffed the bills in his shirt.

She was sealing up the mason jar when she caught me staring at a faint layer of orange dust that lay on the plate where the pills had been. With a sly smile, she licked her index finger and touched it to the powder, then held it up to my mouth. The tip of her finger was lightly flecked with orange.

"Go ahead," she murmured in a husky whisper. I thought it was a joke—there was almost nothing there—but she kept holding it in front of my lips.

"I'm on a diet," I said finally, smiling to cover my nervousness.

She shrugged and licked the tip of her finger herself. Then she plucked a bright-orange pill from her jar and laid it gently inside my breast pocket. "For when you're finished dieting," she said with that same crooked smile.

"What about me?" asked Chris.

She repeated the gesture for Chris, then stashed her jar away and slipped out of the van without saying good-bye.

"Who was that?" asked Chris when she was gone.

"Some chick named Silk. I think she's in college or something."

"Do you have her phone number?" Chris asked. "I'd sort of like to call her."

"I bet you would. What about the grass?" asked Dewy.

"It's fine. We'll take twenty dollars' worth."

Dewy handed the grass to Chris and pocketed his twenty. "You guys want a lift somewhere?"

That van was one cool machine—a regular bedroom on wheels. Curtains, pillows, quadrophonic speakers—even a small refrigerator. We cruised around for a while with the tape deck blaring and Dewy drumming accompaniment on the steering wheel. It was a Hendrix song, one I'd heard before without ever really listening to the lyrics. Jimi posed a new question now, a challenge offered up in a faraway, childlike voice:

> *Have you ever been*
> *Have you ever been to Electric Ladyland?*
> *The magic carpet waits for you*
> *So don't you be late. . . .*

I wanted to ask Chris what he thought it meant, but the van was too noisy for conversation.

We were pretty stoned when Dewy dropped us off in front of Chris's. Luckily there was no one home but Nellie, so we had the run of the house. We were hungry again, so naturally we headed for the kitchen.

"Froot Loops okay?" asked Chris, scanning the cup-board.

"Froot Loops are fine. With milk?"

"Of course with milk."

"Good. That's how I like them."

That got us going in the giggles department. We sat at the kitchen table, staring down at our Froot Loops that bobbed like little red and blue life preservers on a vast white sea of milk. Ridiculous-looking food, if you gave it any thought at all.

"You ever wonder how they get them into neat little rings like this?"

"With a Froot Looper?"

That cracked us up. We were on the floor with giggles when Nellie came in, her arms loaded with freshly laundered sheets.

"I ain't washed that floor yet, so don't y'all go gettin' filthed up like a couple of five-year-olds." That got a big laugh. "And don't be makin' one of your food messes for me to clean up after."

Chris leaped up, grabbed one of her sheets, and draped it over his head like a ghost. Then he ran hooting out of the room. I couldn't resist snatching a sheet and joining in. It was pretty juvenile, I admit, but that sort of thing can be fun if you do it in the right company. We were whipping up and down the stairs, having a wild old time of it. Nellie was hollering bloody murder and chasing around the house after us, but you could tell she wasn't really mad.

When someone yanked the sheet off my head, I reached out and tried to grab it back. But it wasn't Nellie standing over me. It was Mr. Jordan, and he didn't look in any mood for jokes.

"What the hell's going on here?" he asked, grabbing hold of my arm. He wasn't a big guy, but he was plenty strong and had these mean dark eyes.

Just then a sheet-draped figure came flying in from the living room with Nellie in hot pursuit. She pulled up short when she spotted Mr. Jordan, but Chris kept coming. Mr. Jordan stood directly in his path, and Chris barreled straight into him and crashed to the floor, hopelessly tangled in his sheet.

"What the—?" he sputtered, poking his head out through a gaping hole. Then he saw his father and his face fell.

"Come outside a minute, asshole," Mr. Jordan said quietly. "I want to talk to you."

Chris got to his feet, the sheet clenched tightly in his hand. "Well, maybe *I* don't want to talk to *you* . . . asshole!"

I could see the muscles tighten in Mr. Jordan's neck. He glanced over at me and Nellie, like he didn't want company. Nellie scooped up the sheets and disappeared into the kitchen, but I was rooted to the spot.

"I just came from the club," he said in that low menacing voice. "That's where I see my friends and do my business."

"Yeah, well, you're a regular mover and shaker," Chris snarled.

"I'm having a beer after my round of golf when Sammy Howe comes over to say hello. Then he tells me all about the scene you made over there today. Quite a fucking scene, from what he tells me."

"So what?"

"So it's damn embarrassing is what. *I* know what a fuckup you are, but I don't see why you have to advertise it to the world. I didn't even know you were working there."

"You don't know much, do you?"

"I know one thing, buster. If you think you're going to come back here and throw our lives into disarray, you're sorely mistaken. I'll have your ass back in military school faster than you can spit, no matter what your mother says—"

"Keep her out of this. You don't care about her!"

"Look who's talking. Who do—"

"Just shut up, will ya?"

"What was that?" said Mr. Jordan, leaning in close to Chris's face.

"You heard me."

"You've got a big mouth for someone with such an underdeveloped brain. You know what you are? A two-time loser. You couldn't even make it in a second-rate military academy. If you were a stock option, I'd have dumped you years ago and written you off. But you're not so easy to get rid of, are you?"

"Just open the door and I'm gone."

Mr. Jordan reached out his foot and nudged open the front door.

Chris took his exit real slow, keeping his eyes locked on his father's. But when he hit the front lawn he lit off at a gallop. I was still frozen to my spot in the front hall when Mr. Jordan turned his angry glare on me.

That got me unglued—but fast.

Chapter Sixteen

That's how I first found out about Verdant Valley. It was actually just a tract of undeveloped woods half a mile from Chris's house. Construction wouldn't begin for another year, but there was already a big sign perched on the side of the hill:

VERDANT VALLEY:
The Condominium Development
You've Been Dreaming Of

That's where Chris was running to. It turned out he used to go there as a kid to hide out and cool off after fights with his father. He'd even built a clubhouse back in the woods, which is where I found him.

I think he let me follow him there—hell, he could easily have left me in the dust if he'd wanted to. When I finally caught up to him, he was curled up there beside that fallen-down shack. He didn't try to hide the fact that he was crying. He just sat there with his head propped up between his knees, and his face all red and caved in, letting the tears and snot run all together, like a kid who cries without even wiping his face or covering up.

There's not much you can say to someone in a situation like that, so I just slumped down beside him and waited till he was done. Our shoulders were touching, and I could feel him shaking with every fresh wave of sobs. It was quite a while before he stopped, and even then he didn't say anything for a long time. When he finally spoke, his voice was all gravelly and he didn't address me so much as the trees.

"I hate his guts. I've always hated him."

To tell you the truth, it sort of gave me the creeps hearing someone talk like that about his own father, but I wanted him to know I was on his side, so I laid my arm across his shoulders. He leaned into me and wiped his face off on my sleeve, which was pretty gross considering the condition of his face. I didn't mind, but then he tried wiping off my sleeve with his, which only scummed up both our shirts. I had to laugh at that.

"What a mess," he groaned, but he was smiling now.

There was a stream down the slope from the clubhouse, so we stumbled down there to wash. When he peeled off his shirt, the tiny barrel of Orange Sunshine fell out of his pocket onto the ground. It landed neatly on a leaf, shining up at me like a bright penny. I couldn't resist bending down to pick it up.

I let him finish rinsing his face. "Here." I held it out to him. "You dropped this." Then I fished around in my breast pocket and found Silk's other party favor.

I guess that's how it happened. We were both standing there with those little orange pills cradled in our hands. His eyes were still sort of bleary, but they stared straight into mine—not a challenge, really, but an invitation. It seemed the obvious thing to do. We washed them down with creek water.

We didn't know what to expect, so we just stood around for a while and waited for chemistry to take its course.

"Where does this go?" I asked, straining my eyes to follow the path of the creek.

"I don't know." He shrugged. "Through the woods, I guess."

"Yeah, but where?"

"Let's find out," he said, and we headed downstream on opposite sides of the creek.

I have no idea how far we got before I noticed it, but suddenly there's this little man alive inside me, and he's running up and down my spine like it's a keyboard that he's playing scales on. We're walking faster now, as if to keep up with the water as it runs downstream. And then we figure since it's running, we should be too, so we trot alongside it, leaping across whenever it seems right, watching the brook dance below us and listening to the song it's singing in our ears. I can't exactly describe the song, but this stream is definitely singing to me, and it's the most wonderful tune I've ever heard. And I can tell that Chris is hearing it too, because every time I smile over at him, he's smiling back at me the same way.

We pick up the pace as the stream widens, and every time we leap across now, we let out a shout. So as we run and jump and shout, we make our own song to go along with the brook's. And the wind in our ears is a song and the trees standing solemn in the woods are singing too, and all these songs are joined in a sweet chorus, and we know that if we stop running the symphony will stop too, so we keep on running and laughing and shouting till the sunlight itself is a song and the sun on the water sings out to the rocks in the stream, and our hearts thump loudly in rhythm to the beat of our feet on the ground.

And suddenly we're out of the woods and the stream spreads ahead into air—

"Whoa!" Chris shouts, grabbing my arm to keep me from hurtling over the edge of the cliff.

We stop dead, and the music stops with us.

"Look—"

It's silent and beautiful in the sunset as we gaze out over the abandoned quarry.

"Look—"

The stream falls white like a ruffled ribbon, down the canyon to the pool below.

"Look—there—"

And mirrored in the water floor, fifty feet below, are he and me, side by side, pointing back up at us. It makes me dizzy to see us so far away and small. I lean away from the edge and lie down on my back.

The sky is deep deep blue, as in a child's picturebook where the colors first get their names. BLUE. And the leaves on the trees are cut from colored paper, bright and crisp. And the grass—the grass is growing green around my head!

"You ready?" A voice slips through the green.

It's Chris, beside me on the ground.

"You ready?" he asks again, eyeing the rim of the chasm.

"No," I say, without meaning to speak.

He laughs and takes off his belt and makes a loop at one end. Then he takes my hand and pulls me up to him.

"You ready?" Eyes pouring into eyes.

"Yes," I answer, and yes I know I'm ready—finally. Ready to jump, ready to fall.

He loops the belt around my wrist and holds the other end. Ten paces measured from the edge, fear rises and falls away. Then together we break for the quarry, hitting the takeoff cleanly and pumping our legs out over the edge.

One moment of grace before the fall—poised in air, rapt in space—and in that moment frozen forever . . . together.

Then
down
our scream a single falling cry
the wall of water rushing at us like a train
—then through the wall—
CA-BOOOSH!
still sommersaulting down through water
still joined at hands
now up . . . and up . . .
to air and light and smiles laughing
singing like gods . . .
together forever in a sea of laughter.

· · ·

Later, back at the clubhouse, we built a fire to dry our clothes. And as we sat staring into the flame, I knew we'd always be there . . . in that evening . . . together.

And later still, we crouched on his front lawn, like two theives, waiting for the last light to go out. Then he crept inside his house and I went home to mine.

Chapter Seventeen

So naturally, I ended up taking chemistry that summer. And Chris was right—my father was so delighted by my sudden interest in science that he gladly excused me from further job hunting. In his student days he'd spent endless happy hours in university labs probing the edges of life's mysteries. Before going into private practice he'd considered a career in research, a life devoted to the award-winning pursuit of pure science. It hadn't worked out that way for him, but now perhaps his first-born son . . .

Well, Miss Jenkins's summer-school chemistry class wasn't exactly a breeding ground for Nobel laureates. Most of her students had already flunked the course that spring or else needed the extra tutoring before taking it next fall. Of course there were a few nerds who couldn't bear to spend the summer away from school, but they all sat up front taking furious notes on every word out of Miss Jenkins's mouth.

We sat in the back near the only student who interested us—Debbie DeMarco. She was achingly beautiful, and she always wore short cutoffs with a halter top and a delicate silver chain around one of her ankles. That chain really got me. She sat right across the black slate counter from us, but it might as well have been the ocean. It's not that she was unfriendly—she even let me borrow her Erlenmeyer flask once—but I just couldn't imagine how I'd ever break the ice with a girl like that. No way I'd ever have the nerve to pull some rhyming-couplet routine with her. This girl was definitely in another league.

Science wasn't my strong suit, and Chris hadn't progressed very far with his academic attitude, so you can imagine how much serious studying got done. The class was pretty much a goof, and most of our experiments centered on determining the combustion point of our chemistry textbooks when held over a Bunsen burner. We were hoping the smoke might attract Debbie's attention, but it only drew disapproving glares from Miss Jenkins.

By noon each day we had cleaned up our iron filings, packed away our Tinker Toy atomic models, and were off on our bikes to Verdant Valley. We had resolved to rebuild the clubhouse, which basically meant tearing down the ruins of the old one and starting from scratch. The first week was spent scavenging for scrap wood from construction sites around town, which was slow work since we had to carry it all in by hand. We decided to build it into the side of the hill, like a bunker, so it was only visible from the direction of the creek. And when we finished painting it camouflage green, you could only spot it if you knew where to look.

Not that anyone ever wandered through there. But

still, it was our secret place, the only place we really had to hang out together. My parents were none too friendly to Chris, and we tried to stay away from his house when his father was home. So we took the coolest items from our bedrooms and used them to furnish the clubhouse. Chris had a couple of car headlights and an eight-track tape deck he got for his birthday. I donated a dart board and an old sheepskin rug my parents had brought back from Israel. I also found some mismatched squares of carpet in my attic, and Chris dug up a cooler from his basement that was perfect for beer and soda.

We figured a poster or two would polish off the interior decor, so we stopped off at Washington's only head shop one day after class. The Seed was just a hole in the wall next to the Chungking Palace restaurant, but it had a decent collection of posters in addition to the usual hippie paraphernalia. We had just picked out these two very tough Hendrix posters and a black light to go with them when Chris stumbled on the book. *The New Alchemy: Better Living Through Modern Chemistry* was a cheaply printed paperback wedged in between the underground comics and *The Complete Marijuana Cookbook*. Chris read the jacket blurb aloud while I perused a recipe for Cannibas Canapés.

The ancient secrets of mind-expanding substances passed down from the alchemists of old to the psychedelic wizards of tomorrow. For anyone with a year of high school chemistry, the doors of perception are now cast open.

"It's only two bucks," he added. Seemed like a bargain price for the secrets of the ages, so we bought a copy.

We spent the afternoon poring over that book. The New Alchemists were the legendary underground chemists who supplied the counterculture's medicine cabinet. Most of them had fanciful names, like Zach the Wack, who first made Orange Sunshine in a bar in Berkeley, or The Wiz, who imported a million hits of blotter from Ireland soaked into the pages of a Gideon Bible. There were profiles of about a dozen of these characters, followed by recipes for their favorite concoctions—step-by-step directions for the manufacture of White Lightning, Purple Haze, and Green Dragon. It conjured up images of smoking cauldrons and eyes of newt, but there were enough hard figures to make it seem legit.

"Magnesium sulfate," murmured Chris. "Didn't we use that in our pH titration experiment last week?"

"You mean the one you spilled all over our workbook?"

"That's the one. You know, most of this stuff is pretty basic. Maybe we should give it a shot and put all that class time to some practical use."

"Are you serious?"

"Why not? We could be legends in our own time, like, uh . . . Johnny Appleseed."

"Johnny Appleseed?"

"Sure. We could scatter the seeds of cosmic consciousness across the mindfield of America."

"What bullshit. You just want to have the biggest stash on the block."

"We'll be like Benedictine monks, toiling from dawn to dusk making liquor from a mystical formula handed down through the centuries by saints and martyrs. Only we'll call our stock The Third Eye," he continued, pointing to the center of his forehead. "That's what the Hindus call this spot here. It's the eye of God that looks out at the world and in on the soul. Pretty cool, huh?" He drew a sketch of a CBS-style eyeball. "That'll be our signature. What do you think?"

I didn't know what to think. He was all worked up about the idea, but it seemed pretty wild to me. We could barely handle a test tube clamp, much less a complex sequence of commands. But then there was the whole question of destiny, as Chris called it. We never really discussed our first trip, but it felt as if something big began there that afternoon in the woods. What it was, exactly, I couldn't say, but that song still echoed distantly in my mind, and it seemed terribly important that I reconstruct it note for note. It was no mere accident, our meeting Silk and ending up at Verdant Valley that afternoon. Maybe it was all intended: that we should take that trip together, that we should be studying chemistry, that we should stumble on this strange book. And to what end? Perhaps to recover that lost chord and broadcast it out over the world. Who was I to question fate?

"When do we start?" was all I asked.

We started that afternoon, making a list of all the equipment we'd need. The next day we smuggled the first items out of Miss Jenkins's chemistry lab. Just a flask to begin with, followed by a Bunsen burner the next day. Pretty soon we were ferrying a steady stream of paraphernalia from the lab to the clubhouse. Chris insisted that this was a political act, so there was nothing wrong with stealing the stuff, "especially from a public school, which is practically the right arm of the State." I didn't care about all that, but I was afraid of getting caught. One day I thought Debbie saw me slip a triple-beam scale into my satchel, but she didn't say anything about it.

Soon the clubhouse was crowded with equipment, and Chris started buying trade magazines with titles like *Pharmacology Today*. He liked reading the ads.

"Y'know, we're gonna need some cash pretty soon," he said one day.

"No kidding. The cooler's been empty for a week."

"I mean for the lab. There're a few items we have to buy." He tapped his pen against a page in the magazine. "Like this digital gram scale here. Gotta have one of these babies. A hundred and sixteen smackers, plus tax."

"But we've already got a triple beam."

"I'm not gonna cut corners on our signature stock. We're talking micrograms here, so we've got to go with state of the art."

We were riding our bikes home that afternoon when Chris wheeled into a gas station and pulled up beside the Coke machine.

"Listen," he said, still staring straight at the machine, "I want you to go into the office there and tell the guy the machine ate your quarter."

"It's your quarter, you tell him."

"I didn't lose a quarter. I just want you to distract his attention for a minute."

"I don't get it."

"Just do it, will you? I'll explain later."

I shrugged and walked into the office. The mechanic was eating an egg salad sandwich and reading the sports page.

"Excuse me, sir."

"Yeah?" He looked up from his paper. This guy was very ugly.

"I lost a quarter in your Coke machine."

"Nothing wrong with that machine. Just bought one myself." He nodded gruffly toward a grease-smeared Coke can on his desk.

"Well, I put in the quarter and pushed Orange Crush, but nothing came out." I really hate doing that kind of thing, even when I *do* lose a quarter.

"Didja try the coin return?"

"No luck." I shrugged. "And it was my last quarter."

"Your last quarter, huh? Sure it wasn't a slug?" He groaned, and slowly rose to his feet as if in pain. I couldn't help noticing what a big guy he was. Really huge.

I followed him out of the office and around the corner to the machine, but Chris and his bike were gone. What was this, some kind of joke? The mechanic went straight up to the machine and gave it a terrific kick with his boot. He almost knocked the thing over backward.

[124]

"Son of a bitchin' piece a junk," he grunted. "You'd think the bastards would give me a newer model." He grabbed the sides of the machine and shook it fiercely with both hands. "Son of a goddamn bitch!"

I was getting pretty nervous by now and started looking around for an escape route. Out of the corner of my eye I caught sight of Chris slipping into the office. What the hell . . . ?

"Which one dja say ya pushed?"

It was the mechanic, doing an impersonation of a retarded grizzly.

"Uh . . . Coke—I wanted a Coke."

"Thought you said Orange Crush," he growled, grizzly style.

"Did I? Well . . . they're uh . . . they're all the same, really." Stammer City. "Y'know, I'm not even thirsty anymore."

The grizzly took a quarter out of his pocket and dropped it in the slot. "Orange Crush, right?" The name never sounded so menacing.

"Great—swell!"

He bashed the Orange button, and the can thunked out at the bottom. I picked up the can, while he stood and stared at me struggling to flip the top. You know how sometimes you can't get your finger under the tab? Then I finally got it, and it snapped off in my hand.

"What're you, some kinda joker? There's nothing wrong with this machine."

"Oh, I'll just take this home with me . . . I guess . . .

open it there . . . thanks a lot." I was on my bike and hauling out of there in a flash. Chris was waiting for me down the road.

"You know what a jerk you are? I almost got my face rearranged back there." I was really pissed off.

"Relax," he said in a soothing voice. "I was the one taking the risk." He reached into his pocket and pulled out a key ring with two round keys like the kind that fit in bike locks. "Keys to the kingdom." He smiled.

"Where're they from?"

"The office. While you were jawing with King Kong, I waltzed in there and lifted them from his desk."

"And they open . . . ?"

"The Coke machine."

"The Coke machine," I echoed, uncomprehending.

"Where all the quarters live."

I understood now, but I didn't like it. "Great. Terrific. But why bother with Coke machines? Why don't we just knock over a bank?"

"Because banks have armed guards and video cameras."

"You're serious, aren't you? I don't believe this."

"Listen. We can't outfit the lab without cash."

"Which naturally we have to steal."

"So we liberate a few Coke machines, so what?"

"So it's illegal is what."

"So did Robin Hood worry about what was legal or illegal?"

"Robin Hood? Was he related to Johnny Appleseed? What is this, some kind of fairy tale?"

"All right. What do you want to do, bag the whole thing?"

"I just want to stay out of jail."

He glared at me like that was the lamest line he'd ever heard in his life. "You always were a chickenshit when it really counted."

I jumped back on my bike to leave, but he grabbed the front wheel with his hand. "Hey, I'm sorry, I didn't mean that. But Danny-boy, nothing big can happen without taking risks." Then he let go of my wheel.

I could have taken off right then. Maybe I should have, but I didn't want to ride away alone. I wanted to be on the back of his bike again, coasting away from school on the first day of summer vacation.

Looking back, I'm not exactly proud of some of the things I went along with. I could say I got caught up in all the excitement, but the truth of the matter is, I couldn't bear the idea of being left out of any scheme Chris concocted. It's like when you have a favorite movie star and you'll go see any flick he's in, even if it's a Western and you usually hate Westerns. We were well into the second reel by now, and this was one movie I didn't want to watch from the balcony.

Part Three

And so castles made of sand,
slip into the sea,
eventually
> —Jimi Hendrix

Chapter Eighteen

I stayed over at Chris's place that Friday. We figured it'd be easy to slip out of his house unnoticed in the middle of the night. It was. His folks came home from a party around midnight, and from the sound of things they were both pretty tanked. We lay low, and twenty minutes later the house was silent.

Three to five in the morning were our prime poaching hours, when the streets would be virtually deserted. We'd spent the whole week casing the neighborhood—mapping out our route, timing the bike rides between gas stations, noting the location of streetlights. You see, we weren't just hitting the Texaco station. The keys Chris lifted were marked *Series Five*, and half the Coke machines on Linwood Avenue, the main suburban drag, had *Series Five* engraved above their locks. There were twelve *Series Five* stations in all, and only two of them were open all night. The rest were shut down between midnight and six in the morning, but three of those were too close to streetlights for comfort. That left seven, which seemed like a nice round number—almost a mystical number, if you needed that sort of thing for courage.

So it was Friday night and we were lying fully clothed under the sheets in Chris's bedroom. The alarm was set for two-thirty, but there was no way I was drifting off. Chris went over the details in a soft, even voice, but all I could hear was my heart pounding in my chest. Jesus, if I was this shaky lying in bed, how was I going to make it through an actual heist?

"You're the lookout," he said. "That's all you have to do—that and unplug the machine. Got it?"

"Huh?"

"C'mon. We've been through this a dozen times. You have to unplug the machine because it's lit up."

"Right. Right."

"The outside door opens up the refrigerator section. Then the second key opens an inside door that leads to the change tray. That's what we're going for."

"How much do you think we'll get?"

"It's been a hot summer. People have been thirsty."

There was a little knock at the door. *Tap tap tap* like a pen on a desktop.

"It's just my mom," Chris whispered.

We pulled the sheets up over our collars as the door creaked open. Kitty's tiny voice piped through the darkness. "I heard you talking, dear, so I thought . . ."

"C'mon in," he answered as if speaking to a skittish younger sister.

She tiptoed into the room and settled like a bird on the edge of his bed. The hall light spilled in behind her, and she looked even more fragile than I remembered.

"What did you boys do tonight?"

"Hung out, watched TV . . . y'know."

"I just wanted to say good night to you," she said, staring down at her son and pushing the hair off his forehead.

"I know," he replied, so softly I almost didn't hear. "I was waiting for you."

"Well, good night then."

"Good night."

She leaned down and kissed his forehead, then floated noiselessly out of the room.

The alarm clock woke me from a nightmare: I was locked inside a Coke machine and running out of oxygen, and Chris was outside trying to get in, but the key didn't fit the lock. What I remember most is how cold it was inside that machine.

Chris shut off the alarm and rolled out of bed. "It's showtime!" he whispered gaily in my ear.

I was still shivering from the feel of cold aluminum against my skin. Then I realized the bed was drenched with sweat.

Chris touched my shoulder. "Jesus H. Christ—you all right?"

"I'll be fine. Let's go."

We crept downstairs and were almost out the back door when Chris froze in his tracks.

"Damn!" he whispered. "What're we gonna carry the money in?"

"Our pockets?"

"That'd be cute." He held his head in deep thought. "I know."

He crept into the darkened dining room with me right

on his heels. When he got to the credenza, Chris eased open the top drawer. Inside was a large soft bag made of purple velvet. He loosened the drawstring and withdrew a handful of sterling silver knives. They clinked gently against each other, glimmering faintly in the dim light that filtered in from the street. I tried to imagine what we'd say if Mr. Jordan suddenly appeared on the stairway. I couldn't imagine.

Our bikes were waiting outside the back door, and soon we were sailing down tree-lined streets, laughing nervously out loud. The night air felt cool and good against our faces. I was wide awake now and could hear the traffic from Linwood Avenue up ahead, the same way you sometimes hear the ocean surf before you actually get to the beach.

"We should have worn black," Chris muttered. "You should always wear black when you do undercover work at night."

"That's only on television."

"No it's not. My dad says they did it that way in the war. He was with Special Forces in Korea, and he says they always wore black when they went out on secret missions at night, like to mine a bridge or something. They even smeared black shoe polish on their faces."

My father was drafted in the Korean War too, but I couldn't picture him crawling through the night in blackface on his way to blowing up an enemy installation. Actually he was assigned to a base in Texas, where he treated returning G.I.'s for venereal disease. My uncle told me that one night after Thanksgiving dinner.

"Nah, you're right," Chris decided. "We'd probably look suspicious in black. We're just supposed to be two kids on our way to our paper routes."

"At four in the morning?"

"We have to stuff the weekend inserts."

"Right."

Sounded pretty fakey to me, but Chris promised to do the talking if anyone asked. The traffic light on Linwood Avenue was dead ahead now, turning green to red. Was that some kind of omen? A last warning? Chris obviously didn't think so. He turned left through the red light and pulled up across the street from the Shell station. The big yellow sign was shut off, but there was the Coke machine glowing red like a night-light beacon—our first target.

There was almost no traffic on the street. A convertible crammed with teenagers whizzed by. Then nothing for a couple of minutes. Then a slow-moving vehicle with orange parking lights. A cop car? No, just a tow truck hauling a smashed-up sedan behind it.

"Let's move," Chris said when the tow truck had passed. We wheeled across the avenue and dismounted in front of the machine. Chris looked like a Martian as he stood in its deep-red glare.

"Kick the plug," he commanded.

I propped my bike against the cinder-block wall and squeezed around behind the machine to unplug it. The light flicked off and the refrigerating motor wheezed down to silence.

Chris didn't even hesitate. Out came the key. It fit

snugly in the lock, which popped out after a firm twist. Then Chris spun the lock clockwise five or six times and the whole door clicked open. With a "watch this" wink he opened the door wide, revealing six neat columns of soda cans. There must have been a hundred or more of them—Cokes, Orange Crushes, Tabs. They looked sort of deadly, like rounds of ammunition.

"Keep your eye on the street," said Chris as he whipped out the purple bag and fixed the second key into the inside lock. The change tray popped open with a clang.

"Dammit—"

"What's the matter?" I asked, my eyes still fixed on the empty road. The only reply was the sound of the change tray clanging shut, followed quickly by the outer door. He spun the lock closed.

"Plug it back in and let's get out of here."

The plug went in, the machine roared to life, and we scooted away.

"So what's wrong?" I asked when we were clear of the place.

"The change tray was almost empty. I knew it would be when I saw all those cans."

"Meaning they just restocked it?"

"And emptied the money."

"So they could all be empty?"

"There's only one way to find out," he replied grimly.

I'd have been happy to go back to bed then and there, but I knew there was no point even suggesting it.

Esso was next. But their machine's refrigerator was nearly empty of sodas. Chris let out a low whistle as the change tray opened with a distinctly deeper *ker-chunk*.

"Hello, George," he addressed the quarters in a stage whisper. "Home to Martha!" Chris was humming excitedly as we pedaled away from the station.

"How much?" I asked.

"Plenty! Thank you, boys and girls. Keep those quarters coming!" He laughed and tossed me a cold Orange Crush.

Gulf, Arco, Getty and Amoco fell quickly under our assault. The purple bag grew heavy with loot, and my anxiety gave way to mounting euphoria. But we weren't home yet.

"On to Texaco and we're done," Chris announced as the Amoco station receded behind us.

"Let's skip it. That's where we stole the keys, remember?"

"Which means he couldn't have emptied the change tray recently. It's a sure thing." My panic returned as soon as we pulled up under the big red Texaco star.

"Please, Chris. Don't we have enough?"

"Hey, I've got this down to a science. I'll be in and out in a flash."

It's true, he'd gotten very agile with those keys. He was already spinning the lock and swinging open the door as he spoke.

The inside bulb flooded out on us like a searchlight— I'd forgotten to unplug it!

Chris slammed the door shut with a loud clang. As if in response, a light shot on inside the gas station office. A dog began barking.

"Let's go, let's go!" I whisper-shouted, panic rising in my throat.

"I can't get the key out—the lock's jammed!"

"So leave it!" I grabbed the money sack and hopped onto my bike.

"Wait—I think I've got it. . . ."

King Kong came lumbering out of the office leading a Doberman pinscher on a choke leash. You know, one of those dogs that eat live baby rabbits for breakfast.

"Eh—eh—ah—!" was all I could manage.

Chris looked up and caught sight of our hosts.

"Be cool," he said as he stepped in front of the lock, where the jammed keys still dangled.

"What the hell's going on out here?" yelled Kong, only five yards away now.

"We're . . . we're—we're paperboys!" I yelled too loudly. I admit I lost my cool. The Doberman barked louder and foamed at the mouth.

"Stay right where you are," commanded Kong.

It was too late to run for it—he was already blocking our escape. Did he recognize me? No, it was still dark and my back was to the red light.

"We—we have to insert our stuffings," I blustered. I could hear Chris moan behind me.

Kong strode right up and peered into our faces. "Step away from there," he barked. Chris inched reluctantly away from the lock. When Kong saw the key ring, he quickly grabbed hold of Chris's jacket.

"What've you punks—?"

As he spoke, I whipped around with the money sack like an Olympic hammer thrower. It was an instinctive reaction, but I surprised myself. The bag sailed right past Kong's ear and crashed through the plastic COKE sign on the front of the door. Fluorescent tubes imploded noisily, enveloping Kong in a cloud of red smoke.

"Now!" cried Chris as he retrieved the bag and leaped aboard his bike. I didn't need any prompting—I was already pedaling furiously out of the lot.

Something grabbed my bike and yanked it to a halt.

I looked down to find the Doberman's jaws clamped firmly around my rear wheel and the air hissing out between his bared fangs. I was about to abandon my bike and flee on foot when a soda can sailed through the air from Chris's direction and caught the dog squarely on the nose.

With a loud yelp, he released the tire and scurried back to his master. I was out of there in a flash, the flattened tire thumping frantically in rhythm with my heartbeat.

"Insert our stuffings!" Chris hooted, still pumping like crazy down the back streets. "Hah! I love it!"

"That was supposed to be your line! Where were you?" But I was too relieved to be angry.

"You should have seen your face when that dog chomped your tire. It was priceless!"

"That could've been my foot."

"Could've been your ass!"

It was almost light out when we crept back into Chris's house and upstairs to his room. I collapsed exhausted on the bed, but the sight of the bulging bag of coins brought me around pretty quick. Chris hefted the sack for weight, then casually untied the drawstring and inverted it over the bed. The loot poured out in a clattering stream of silver, making an awesome mountain of coins, like in a fairy tale. We were both stunned for a moment, but soon we were laughing and running our hands through the pile like a couple of Rumpelstiltskins.

Finally we quieted down and set about counting the loot. It took us a long time, but we didn't mind. The grand total was 1,384 quarters, 840 dimes, 623 nickels and 2 brass slugs. But the whole time we were counting, I kept replaying that scene in my head when I'd tried to clobber that guy with the sack of coins. A total stranger, and I'd almost killed him over the contents of a god-damn Coke machine. Jesus H. Christ.

Chapter Nineteen

The guy at the chemical supply store gave us a funny look when we paid for the digital gram scale with five hundred quarters.

"What'd ya do, break the piggy bank?" he asked as he counted out the coins four at a time.

"Actually, I won at poker," replied Chris. "An ace-high flush bet into my full house. Never saw it coming, the poor sap."

I was worried that we'd have to show some identification, but Chris simply told the salesman we were working on a science project for school and gave a fake name for the receipt.

Next stop was the hardware store, where we picked up a power generator, water pump, and hose. By the end of our shopping spree we were so loaded down, we spent our last five bucks on a cab.

"You want to get off *here*?" asked the cabbie when we told him to pull over by the Verdant Valley sign.

"We're going fishing, okay?" said Chris irritably.

"With all that gear?"

"What're you, a game warden?"

We made sure the cab was out of sight before setting

out into the woods. No one knew about our hideout, and every week we rerouted the path through the woods so it wouldn't get too worn. We also made a huge thicket fence out of branches to prop in front of the lab each day when we left. The only way you could spot our compound now was from a low-flying aircraft, but all we ever saw was an occasional traffic copter.

Chris wasn't very mechanically minded, so I played hooky that week and converted the clubhouse to a lab while he went to classes. I'd helped my father set up a darkroom in our basement once, so I knew something about building sinks and running hose from a pump. I found a fifty-gallon oil drum to use as a holding tank, so I didn't have to run water all the way from the creek. Wiring the generator for electric light was a little trickier, but I bought a how-to manual from Sears and figured it out. I couldn't wait for Chris to get back from class that day and see the lightbulb blazing in the lab.

It was a hot afternoon, so I stripped off my shorts and lay in the creek with my head resting on a flat rock. The sun was beating down on my body through the cool water, the locusts were making their summer noises, and I was thinking about the cold quart of beer that Chris had promised to bring out with him. But beer wasn't all he brought along that day.

"Watch out for the poison ivy over there."

It was Chris, coming through the brush. But who the hell was he talking to?

"That's okay," answered a girl's voice. "It can't hurt you unless it senses your fear."

"That right?"

"I read it in a magazine, I don't remember which one."

When they stepped into the clearing, I was still lying bare-assed in the creek. I couldn't believe he'd brought some chick here. And I couldn't believe I'd left my pants up the slope by the lab. Jesus.

"Hey, there, nature boy," Chris called out like there was nothing unusual about showing up there with a girl. "We've got company."

"Oh, and you have a beautiful stream!" she cooed, skipping down to the creek and kneeling to dip her hand in the water about three yards away from me.

I rolled over onto my stomach. I was too embarrassed to look her in the eye, but I couldn't help noticing the little silver chain wrapped around her ankle. It was Debbie DeMarco.

"Hi." She smiled, as if seeing me for the first time.

I glared up at Chris, but he pretended not to notice.

"You know Debbie from chemistry class, don't you?" he asked.

"Welcome to Verdant Valley," I said, my voice thick with sarcasm.

"Christopher's told me all about what you're doing here. It's so exciting."

"Christopher's quite a talker."

As you've probably noticed by now, Chris had a way with the ladies. Not that he worked at it or anything. It just came naturally to him, like catching a football or sinking a basket. And it wasn't hard to see why. For starters, his hair had grown out to full black ringlets, so he looked like one of those nineteenth-century drawings of a Greek youth. And he had those dark flashing eyes and a winning smile. And like I said before, he looked good when he moved.

Whatever it is that turns girls on, Chris had it in spades. But it wasn't just his looks. He had a genuine nonchalance around girls, like he barely noticed or cared if they were there. But when he finally got around to looking one in the eye, he could bowl her over backward. And he didn't need any poems or flower gimmicks. Most guys wouldn't want to compete with that kind of charisma, but I figured some of his magnetism might rub off on me. Maybe it was something I could catch, like a cold.

"Come check out the lab," called Chris. As Debbie turned to climb the slope, he tosed me my cutoffs. I scrambled out of the creek and into my pants.

"Hey, look—a light!" He'd discovered my handiwork.

"Looks more like a darkroom than a lab," said Debbie.

"That's because we haven't set up the equipment yet," I answered, a little peeved.

But as soon as she turned and looked at me, my tough-guy routine was shot to hell. That's what certain kinds of girls do to me—everything in the back of my throat turns to mush so I'm practically gagging on my own tongue and I can't swallow or form words with more than one syllable. Well, Debbie was that kind of girl—she had the type of perfect body I'd only seen in maga-zines, but with even softer edges. You couldn't really say where one part of her left off and another started, if you know what I mean. Except for her eyes, which were crystalline blue, like bright flowers. I know it's a corny image, but that's what her eyes were like—tiny blue flowers with bursts of yellow in the centers.

"I really admire people who can build things." She smiled through her gorgeous blond mane. Did I mention her hair? For a minute I forgot to be mad at Chris. For a minute I forgot my name, forgot what year it was.

"Danny-boy's a regular master builder, aren't you?" said Chris. As if to punctuate his question, he leaned backward and rested his head on Debbie's shoulder. All my elation quickly evaporated as I watched her twirl her fingers idly through his hair. How could she resist?

But in a minute she was skipping back down to the creek bed and wading in with her bare feet. "Too bad it's such a shallow stream," she murmured, almost to herself. "It'd be great for skinny-dipping."

I should have known I was in trouble right there, because my mind was already racing ahead to the problem of how to carve a swimming hole out of that crummy little creek. Maybe if I dredged it and dammed it up . . .

When she finally left and my brain returned to a functional mode, I lit into Chris. But my heart wasn't in it.

"Don't get me wrong," I said, "I can't argue with your taste. Hell, I hope she has a sister. But why'd you have to bring her up here and blow our cover? Wasn't there some other way you could impress her? Couldn't you take her home and show her your stamp collection?"

He seemed to find my tirade amusing. "You're way off base. I brought Debbie out here because we need what she's got."

"Of course we do. I've been needing that since sixth grade."

"Not that, you sex fiend. This." He tapped the side of his head. "She just so happens to be the best student in the class."

"She is?"

"A regular prodigy!" He was laughing now. "And when I mentioned to her that I was working on an extracurricular project, she was full of ideas and suggestions. She's dying to help."

"But can we trust her?"

"Relax. I sounded her out on the subject before I spilled anything. She's cool, believe me."

"But I don't see why we need her."

"Listen man, this isn't aspirin we're making here. I mean, there're highly flammable chemicals involved."

"I thought we were partners, Chris. Just you and me."

"Sure we are. We need a little outside assist here is all."

I didn't mean to whine, but I smelled trouble. How could anyone be interested in Debbie just for her brain? I sure couldn't. And when it came to the rest of her body, I knew I couldn't compete with Chris. I didn't want to compete with him—or with her.

Then one day Chris didn't show up at class. When I caught up to him that afternoon at Verdant Valley, he was sitting down by the stream, just staring into the water. He looked up and I saw he had a black eye. But he wouldn't talk about it, except to say it was a present from his father.

That kind of broke the spell of our summer idyll. Suddenly Chris was in a big hurry to start production. He wanted to give it a shot right off, but Debbie convinced him to wait till we were ready. I worked every day putting the finishing touches on the lab. And every evening they studied late together over at her house. At least that's what they said they were doing.

Chapter Twenty

It was later that week when Chris called me at home after dinner.

"We're on the guest list at Emergency tonight to hear The Heathens. I'll look for you out front at ten."

Emergency was a local rock club, and The Heathens were the group Dewy drummed for. I expected to find Debbie there with him, but Chris was waiting alone at the door. He thumped me happily on the back, then turned to the bouncer leaning against the $5 COVER sign.

"We're on the guest list," said Chris. "Two for Jordan."

The bouncer peered down at a half-lit list of names. "I spilled some tequila on this, so the names are sort of soggy."

"We're down there, believe me. Friends of Dewy's."

"Hey, I believe ya, but unless I can find your name—ah, forget it." He stamped the backs of our hands with invisible ink and waved us inside.

Emergency was your classic fire trap. A narrow, low-ceilinged den of a club with no ventilation and virtually no light. No tables or chairs either—everyone just lay out on the floor or leaned up against the Day-glo-painted walls that shook with overamplified music. As we wandered through the club, disembodied voices hissed out at us from darkened corners: "Acid, mesc, hash, grass. Acid, mesc, hash, grass."

"So what're we doing here?" I yelled over the din. "This place gives me the creeps."

"We've got some business with Dewy," he shouted back.

The band was crashing through their first set onstage. The Heathens were a good match for their names, but their problem wasn't their look, it was their music. All they had was raw energy, with the accent on raw. We could see Dewy up there pounding hell out of his drums, but no one was dancing or even clapping their hands. At Emergency the music was strickly background. The main event was getting wasted.

At the end of the set we made our way backstage, which was no big deal—just a trashy room with bare lightbulbs, cracked walls, and broken-down old furniture. And of course The Heathens. They were hanging around with that vacant-eyed look you get from standing too close to amplifiers for too long. The lead guitarist was bitching to the sound man about the mike feeds while the bass player smoked a joint with a girl who looked about twelve years old.

Dewy sat on a couch with a mirror balanced on his lap, chipping away at a white crystal the size of a golf ball.

"Hey, dudes, how's tricks?" he called as he snorfled up a line of dust. "You want a taste of this rock? Pure meth. Got it off some motorcycle gang in Trenton. I can get it for you at twenty a spoon or forty a gram. It'll tear your eyes out—promise."

That didn't strike me as a very tempting offer, but Chris wasn't one to turn down free speed. He did a line.

"Funny us running into each other like this," said Dewy as he went back to chipping the rock. "I was just thinking of giving you guys a call."

"Dewy, I called you," said Chris.

"You did?"

"Yeah, and you put us on your guest list."

Dewy bobbed his head to one side like someone shaking water out of his ear. "Oh, right. I remember. Something about . . . don't tell me . . . oh yeah, oh yeah. Something about an acid connection."

"We've got a direct line to the lab," said Chris. "I can get you all you want."

"That a fact, that a fact . . ." mumbled Dewy. He turned the thought over in his mind, which must have been quite a task in his condition. "Why don't you gentlemen step into my office."

If you've never been in the backstage bathroom of a down-and-dirty rock den, you haven't missed much. That was Dewy's "office." Really nothing to write home about. When we entered, two kids of indeterminate age and sex were groping around inside one of the doorless stalls.

"Hey, people," Dewy addressed them firmly, "we need this space, okay?" The pair stumbled out into the hallway. Dewy leaned his back against the door and

Blairsville High School Library

grinned across at us. There was something seriously wrong with his gums.

"You cats are in luck. My main man in Baltimore just got busted and his whole operation's shut down. I'll handle any quantity you can pass along . . . *if* I get it by Fourth of July weekend."

"What's happening on the Fourth?"

"Where've you dudes been? The Grateful Dead is giving a free concert on the monument grounds. Every freak on the east coast will be here, and those Dead Heads are oinkers when it comes to acid. They eat the stuff for breakfast."

"Great. July Fourth is no problem," Chris assured him.

"That's only a week from now. I can't use 'em after that."

"Consider it done."

"And it's got to be pure stuff, or it's no go. There's plenty of competition in this marketplace, let me tell ya."

"I said there's no problem."

"And could you do 'em up with some groovy design? Y'know, like, uh, pyramids or stars or some shit like that? Customers get a kick out of it, makes it easier to move."

"Sure thing, Dewy. We've got that all worked out. Now, can we talk numbers?"

"Sure, I'll talk numbers. Six thousand hundred zillion zotnoids to the eighth logarithmic power." He collapsed into giggles. "Now you talk some numbers."

"Here's what we had in mind," said Chris evenly, trying to keep things businesslike. "We'll deliver hundred-hit sheets of blotter—you can slice 'em up any way you like. We want thirty bucks a sheet up to five hundred sheets."

"What if I take a thousand?"

"Sheets?" asked Chris. "Just a sec." He snapped up a piece of soap from the sink and scrawled some figures on the mirror. I noticed his hand shaking a little, but that could have been the speed.

"You want a thousand sheets?" he asked, stalling for time while he reran the numbers.

"If the price is right."

"Second set's starting, Dew!" someone shouted through the door.

"Be right there," he called back, still staring straight at Chris.

"Okay, okay," said Chris. "Twenty-five . . . call it twenty thousand dollars."

Dewy's eyes rolled upward toward some innercranial calculator. "If you can deliver a thousand sheets by the Fourth, I'll take 'em off your hands for ten g's."

"Ten thousand dollars? On delivery?"

"On delivery."

Chris drew me into an empty stall. "Whattaya think?"

"Why ask me? You seem to be doing fine by yourself."

"Hey, don't be like that. Whattaya think?"

I shrugged. "Seems like a lot of money."

Chris nodded his agreement and signaled okay to Dewy. They sealed the deal with another line of speed.

"It's been a pleasure doing business, guys," said Dewy as he leaned across the sink and rinsed off the mirror.

"But, right now"—he popped an unmarked black capsule into his mouth—"I gotta go beat my skins."

Chris was flying when we left the club. He wanted to celebrate, so we decided to head for Howard Johnson's. That's the problem with being a teenager. When grown-ups want to celebrate something, they walk right into a bar and order champagne. Or else they go to some swank restaurant and have a French meal with a twenty-year-old bottle of wine. The only place we could come up with was Howard Johnson's.

I didn't care that night, though, because I wasn't in the mood for celebrating. I wanted to slow everything down, turn it back a few weeks, and start over. But instead of slowing down, things seemed to be speeding up every second.

"Ten thousand begonias!" Chris hooted under his breath as we slid into opposite sides of an orange banquette. "A man can buy a lot of fried clams with that sort of moolah."

"The clams here are frozen, you know. I'll bet they probably dug them out of some contaminated clam bed about ten years ago, and popped 'em in the deep freeze. A decade later they toss 'em into a vat of grease, and presto—Chris's delight!"

"You know that's bullshit. What's wrong with you?"

"Nothing."

"What's your problem, anyway?"

I pretended to study the menu for a minute. "You never mentioned selling the stuff."

"What else would we do with it?"

"I thought we were gonna give it away."

"Yeah, well . . . people don't value what they don't pay for."

"Like Johnny Appleseed, you said."

Now it was his turn to study the menu. "And anyway, I could use the bread."

"What for?"

"You boys decided what you want yet?" It was our waitress, a middle-aged woman in a bright-orange uniform with thick-soled white shoes. She looked like a nurse in a citrus tree hospital.

"We'll have two plates of fried clams and a couple of root beer floats with vanilla ice cream," Chris ordered, grinning perversely across the booth at me.

"You want the clam strips, or clams with bellies?" she asked.

"Oh, belly up I guess. And could you bring us some extra tartar sauce with that? Thank ya, darlin'."

The waitress plodded off, her moon shoes squishing underfoot.

"Listen," he said, leaning across the booth toward me, "things have gotten really heavy for me at home."

"What happened?"

"It seems my father's found a military academy hard up enough to take me. In fucking Tuskaloosa, Alabama, if you can believe it."

"Damn."

"So . . . I guess it's about time I made tracks."

"Made tracks where?"

"I was thinking about Colorado. I could get a job at a ski resort."

"But Chris, it's the middle of summer."

"That's why I need the bread. I figure I could camp out till the first snow, then look for a job on the slopes." He chewed intently on the end of his straw. "I was hoping you'd come along."

"I don't ski."

"So I'll teach you," he said hopefully. "It'll be a gas."

The waitress delivered our root beer floats and waddled away. *Squish squish squish.*

"What about Debbie?" I asked.

"What *about* Debbie?"

"Is she coming along?"

"Nah. Why complicate things with a woman?"

"Does she know about this?"

"No."

"You gonna tell her?"

"No." A beat. "But don't worry. She'll get her cut."

The waitress returned with our food.

"*Two* fried clam platters, *with* bellies—extra tartar on the side!" she announced loudly. We ignored her and she went away.

Chris stared intently down at the float, which he stirred with his straw. "So, uh . . . whattaya say, buddy? You with me?"

I only hesitated a moment. I didn't want to give my mind a chance to get in the way.

"Yeah, man. You know I am."

Chris smiled warmly at me, then turned his gaze to the steaming plates of fried clams. "That's what I love about these suckers," he said in a hearty voice. "They always look just like the photo on the menu. Right down to the little green specks in the tartar sauce." He peered down at the sauce. "What is that green shit, anyway? Never mind—I'd rather not know."

Chapter Twenty-One

I don't know why I agreed to take off with Chris like that. The whole idea was screwy—running away to Colorado and hiding out like a couple of outlaws till the snows came. But just then, when he proposed it over root beer floats, the wilderness sounded safe and simple— like a new Verdant Valley—somewhere we could spread our wings and soar beyond the reach of parents and schools. I wanted to believe we could make a fresh start and take care of each other there. And more than that, I wanted to say yes to him. I wanted to hear myself say, "You know I'm on your side, buddy," and see him smile in response.

Things weren't so great at home for me either. I'd been fighting quite a bit with my parents lately. Not over anything in particular but everything in general: the length of my hair, the clothes I wore, the kids I hung out with, meaning Chris. Mostly I fought with my mom. We'd start in bickering over something stupid till gradually we worked our way up to a full-tilt screaming match. My father hung back and waited till things got nasty before stepping in to break it up. From time to time he'd take me aside and try to give me tips on how to deal with my mother, man-to-man stuff like: "Women are hysterical creatures—always keep that in mind, Son." But I wasn't interested in his advice. I knew whose side he was on when the chips were down.

Things being how they were, the idea of running away with Chris had definite appeal. But that particular weekend I was supposed to go to the seashore with my family. I tried to duck it, but my parents weren't about to leave me home alone, even for a weekend. So Friday afternoon we packed up the car and drove to the beach.

It turned out to be your basic hassle-filled family weekend with the usual share of hurt feelings on both sides. Then early Sunday morning, just before dawn, my father shook me awake and gestured silently to the fishing rod in his hand. "Don't wake your brother," he whispered. Mark was sound asleep in the bed beside me.

I was too sleepy to complain about being wakened at dawn. My father's practically an insomniac, so it's nothing for him to get up that early. But I'm more of a night person—I like to sleep in whenever I can. Anyway, I stumbled around in the dark getting dressed and met my father outside by the car.

We didn't talk much on the drive out to Lasky's Point. I was still half asleep, and my father's not a big talker anyway. He's more of a thinker. With some quiet people you figure they're just listening to the radio or watching the road go by. But with my father you definitely get the feeling he's thinking, and not just about what he ate for breakfast.

It was barely dawn when we got to the Point, and the

sun was coming up a big red ball over the ocean. It was really spectacular, I have to admit. It almost made me glad to be awake. That's why my father likes to fish there first thing in the morning, because it's so pretty. He claims the fish are running best at dawn, but I've never seen him actually catch anything. It's almost a family joke, his never catching anything. He doesn't seem to mind, though. He just likes to stand there in the surf and cast out and reel in and cast out again.

That's the best thing about surf casting—it's so simple you don't even have to mess with bait. You just tie a lure to the end of line, wade out a ways, and cast. Of course every summer my father goes into the Bait 'n' Tackle shop and has a long talk with the owner about which lures the fish are biting that year. And he always buys one or two new ones, but that's part of the joke. "I'll take a couple of those Flying Dutchman spinners on your say-so, Mr. Giles." He does it all with a totally straight face, too, which is why it's so funny.

Anyway, we were the only guys on the beach that morning, since all the real fishermen knew better than to fish the Point. We only had one rod, so mostly I just sat on the beach watching the sea gulls and hunting around for shells. Then I took a few casts while my father coached me. "Straighten your elbow. That's it. Now get your shoulder into it." The whole thing was one long inside joke.

Well, I was having a good time seeing how far I could cast, trying to keep my elbow straight and arc the lure way out over the breakers. I wasn't thinking about much, just enjoying the morning sun and the feel of the surf on my legs, when—*ZWAAP!*—I get this monster strike. At first I didn't even realize what was happening. I'd never gotten a nibble before, much less a real bite. I figured I must have fucked up and snagged a buoy or something. But my father knew right away that I'd hooked a fish. He was jumping up and down in the surf shouting instructions at me.

"Give 'em line, give 'em plenty of play!"

Well, I froze up immediately. He'd told me a dozen times before what to do when a fish strikes, but I'd never bothered to listen. Now there was some whale on the end of my line and I was supposed to land him.

Relax. I'm not gonna bore you with a whole long fish story here. If you want to read about that stuff, go buy a Hemingway novel. He does it a whole lot better than I can. Personally, I think it's corny as hell—father and son battle fish—and that's not the point of the story, anyway. But to finish with the fish: After about twenty minutes of me freaking out and my father shouting instructions, I managed to land the sucker. And yes, it was a beaut—a twenty pounder—and yes, I got a huge rush from seeing this humongous bluefish lying on the sand at the end of my line.

But the *point* of the story is that my father was even more excited than me. The whole way home he was going on and on about what a thrill it was to watch me land it and all. I mean you'd think after so many summers of getting up at dawn and buying expensive tackle and taking endless ribbing from family and friends, you'd think he'd be just a little pissed off that I was the one who finally caught the fish. But he was really happy for me, and I could tell he wasn't just faking it.

We went home and woke everyone up and showed off the fish. Then we took pictures of it and cleaned it and filleted it and barbecued it, for chrissake. But it wasn't till that afternoon when we were sitting around the table and I bit into my first salty mouthful—that's when it really hit me. *These* people weren't the enemy, they were just my family—my parents and my brother. Sure they were a pain in the ass to live with, but at least they cared about me. So what if we fought a lot? I wasn't made of glass.

And if I ran away to Colorado, I'd miss out on driver education that fall. My parents kept saying I was too immature to get a license, but I had the feeling they might give in as my birthday got closer and they realized all the carpooling it would save them. And I was about due for a new ten-speed racer, which could probably be arranged, since sixteen is sort of an important birthday. Then of course there was Thanksgiving, always my personal favorite in the holiday department. Maybe Chris and I could trap a turkey in the wild, but I wouldn't have a clue about cooking it. And what about the stuffing?

And then there was the whole question of school. It'd be great to spend autumn outside a classroom for a change, and I wouldn't shed any tears over missing out on geometry or biology. But if I dropped out now, I could kiss college good-bye. I didn't care about the degree or anything, but I had this picture stuck in my head of me as a college freshman with all sorts of cool buddies and a foxy girlfriend—or even two—and maybe a beard. I know it sounds stupid, and of course it hasn't worked out that way, but what did I know back then? All I knew was I wasn't ready to leave it all behind yet. And when I suddenly realized I didn't have to, the relief washed over me like a cool breeze—a wonderful feeling of peace and well-being.

Now all I had to do was convince Chris to stick around. It would take some doing, but I could be pretty persuasive when I wanted to be. There were all sorts of solutions. Maybe we could get an apartment downtown. Maybe we could take off for a month of camping and be back in time for school. I'd figure something out. In the meantime, there was this awesome piece of baked bluefish that required my attention.

Chapter Twenty-Two

I was still feeling fine when I got home late Sunday. But I awoke Monday morning to find that my sense of calm had fled in the night. And when I called Chris's house and he wasn't there, my panic swelled. I vaulted onto my bike and sprinted out to Verdant Valley, running and out of breath by the time I reached the lab.

At first the place looked deserted, but then I noticed Debbie crouched on a blanket down by the stream. She was kneeling, with her long blond hair thrown over her head to dry in the sun. She didn't have any top on, and her shoulders still glistened with droplets of water. I stood there watching, waiting for her to look up and notice me. But she didn't, so I kept watching, I guess for longer than I should have. Finally, she sat up, pushing her hair back with both hands. When she saw me, she leaped off the blanket and pulled it around her.

"Danny—you gave me a start," she said with a nervous little laugh. "I was just . . . washing my hair. You know what they say about fresh spring water."

"Yeah. . . . I, uh, was looking for Chris."

"You just missed him."

"Oh . . . well."

She looked around for her shirt. "He went into town to buy some supplies. Chemicals, that sort of thing. You know how eager he is to get this show on the road."

"Right, right." I saw her halter top lying behind a rock, but I didn't point it out. "So you guys got here early today."

"Well, actually . . . we camped out last night."

"Oh yeah?" I couldn't keep the quaver out of my voice.

"Yeah. It was fun. I'd been wanting to do it, and Chris—Chris was happy to get out of his house. You know."

"Yeah, I know."

What did I know? Nothing. I didn't know a damn thing! But I was wising up fast. Suddenly I knew that I wasn't talking Chris out of anything. If I didn't go along with him, he'd take Debbie instead. She was already getting that possessive, womanly glint in her eye.

She found her halter and put it on with her back to me. While I watched her, something cold and hard rose up in my throat. Something mean that hurt and wanted to hurt back.

She was brushing out her hair now, langorous and easy. "I'm worried about him, Danny," she said between strokes. "The way he fights with his father, I'm afraid he'll do something to hurt himself."

So he hadn't told her yet. But soon he would—maybe tonight. I had to do something, now.

I lay down against the bank and stared at the sky,

letting a few clouds pass before making my move. "I'm gonna miss this spot," I said absently.

"We can come here all fall. It'll be beautiful when the leaves change."

"Right . . . right," I corrected myself.

But she snatched up the bait. "Why are you going to miss this place?"

"Forget it."

She crawled up the bank beside me. "What did you mean?"

"I thought he'd have told you by now. He said he was going to."

"Tell me what?" Her voice already had a scared edge to it. I let her sweat it out for a few seconds before answering.

"Well, why do you think he's in such a rush to make the acid?"

"I don't know. I guess he wants some distraction from the other stuff, the stuff with his father."

"What do you think *you* are?" That just slipped out.

"Would you mind telling me what you're getting at?" She tugged at my shoulder, getting riled now. "And look at me when you talk."

I rolled over on my side and faced her. I realized I'd never had the nerve to look her straight in the eye before.

"Chris is leaving town—heading out to Colorado."

That took the wind out of her sails.

"But—he can't do that."

"Why not?"

"Don't you see? He's just running away from his pain. He'll get into some kind of trouble."

"He'll be okay." A beat for good measure. "I'm going with him."

She was getting the picture now. I could see it spread across her face the way a ripple blooms on the surface of a pond. I'd set the clock ticking, ticking down to . . .

"What about—what about school . . . and your families?" What about her, she meant.

"It's all set. We've already arranged to sell the acid, so we'll have plenty of bread to get out there and settled in."

"But I thought we were giving it away."

"People don't value what they get for free," I parroted. "And don't worry, you'll get your cut." That made her wince, and I was suddenly sorry I'd said it.

"When is he . . . when are you planning to leave?"

"As soon as we make the stuff and do the deal. In a week, I guess." I got to my feet. "But listen, don't tell Chris about this, okay? I'm sure he means to fill you in himself."

As I left the clearing, I glanced back and saw Debbie just as I'd found her, collapsed over her knees again, her hair a thick blond curtain around her face.

What I did next was I went home and mowed the lawn. That's how bent out of shape I felt. I mean, I *hated* mowing the lawn. We had this big old Toro that weighed about twenty tons and made a terrible racket. Battling that monster was a sure way to ruin your afternoon. But my day was already shot, and I didn't want to think about it.

So I pushed that sucker back and forth across the lawn, breathing in the smelly fumes and staring straight ahead at the patch of grass in front of the mower. The engine roared in my head, chasing out everything else, which was fine by me. I finished the front lawn and moved to the back. I revved the engine higher and pushed the mower harder. More fumes and more noise and— *THWACK!*—the rotor blade cracked against a rock and the engine sputtered to a halt. I stood there in the sudden quiet, choking on the fumes and fighting back my tears.

I bolted onto my bike and pedaled furiously back out to the lab, my mind racing. Was it possible? Had I really crossed up my best friend over some girl? Who was I kidding anyway? I didn't care as much about Chris as I did about me. *My* friend, *my* future. I'd made good and sure things worked out *my* way—and I hated myself for it.

I don't know what I expected, but I wasn't surprised to smell smoke when I ditched my bike and charged into the woods. As I neared the clearing, I could see the flames through the trees.

I found Chris on his knees, not far from where I'd left Debbie. But she was gone and the lab was engulfed in fire. Strange chemical flames danced pink and blue along the rooftop, flickering dully against Chris's face.

"She torched it," he said blankly without looking up. "She ruined everything."

I pulled him to his feet.

"Listen, man, we better get out of here. This is gonna draw a crowd."

"Why would she do that? Last night she said she loved me."

I led him away from the inferno and back through the woods. Someone had called the fire department, and we could already hear the sirens wailing toward us as we mounted our bikes and rode off.

Chapter Twenty-Three

Going to the concert was my idea. Chris was totally apathetic about it once the lab burned down, but I thought it might cheer him up.

"C'mon, buddy, it's the Fourth of July—Declaration of Independence, revolutionary war—your kind of stuff. Not to mention drugs, sex, and rock 'n' roll."

I couldn't get a smile out of him, but he finally agreed to go.

Ordinarily, the Fourth of July is my least favorite holiday. It always seems to be a hundred degrees outside, and I have to spend the afternoon with my family at the Kesslers' barbecue. But that day I was in pretty good spirits. Somehow, despite all my fears, things had turned out okay. Chris's dream of escaping to Colorado had literally gone up in smoke, and somewhere along the way I'd even shaken Debbie off our backs. Of course there was still Chris's father to deal with, but together we could face anything. What were friends for, after all? I was hoping we could have a good time together at the concert and make a fresh start of things.

After the barbecue, I picked up Chris and we rode our bikes downtown together. The Grateful Dead were famous for their outdoor gigs, and since this was a free concert, they were sure to draw a big crowd. The sun had just set when we arrived at the Washington Monument, but there were already tens of thousands of fans spread out on blankets across the lawn.

"I bet they don't have scenes like this in Colorado," I said, trying to inject some gaiety into Chris's somber mood.

We surveyed the crowded grounds from the Monument's knoll. Frisbees flew randomly through the air, joints and jugs of wine passed freely in all directions, and everywhere you looked folks were dancing up a storm—and the music hadn't even started yet. Then a local group, The Machine, came onstage and the crowd rose to its feet in greeting. The whole energy level jumped an octave as the band launched into its first song.

I cracked a couple of beers and passed one to Chris, but he was too restless to drink it. "Listen, I'm gonna go score us some goodies," he said, scanning the crowd for a likely source.

"C'mon man," I tried to dissuade him. "We've already got a couple of ludes and a joint."

But he was determined to stock up, and he'd come to the right place for it. The grounds were crawling with Dewys, offering a full spectrum of mind-altering substances at bargain prices—uppers, downers, twisters and scramblers, organic or synthetic. A regular holiday clearance sale.

"I'll be back in a flash," he said, and headed off into the crowd.

Two hours later he hadn't returned.

A full moon rose behind the bandstand, casting a pale white light over the increasingly aroused assembly. The Washington Monument, a cold white shaft in the moonlight, towered overhead like a lightning rod drawing atmospheric energy to the spot.

Things continued to heat up through the evening, and when the Grateful Dead mounted the stage around eleven, everyone seemed to take that as a cue to polish off whatever remained of their drug stashes. By the middle of the set, the general level of dementia had risen considerably. I wasn't exactly cold sober myself, but the vibe had definitely tilted in a deranged direction. There seemed to be an unusual number of people racing aimlessly through the crowd shrieking at the top of their voices. And every twenty minutes an announcement came over the P.A. system about some bad acid that was going around. "Don't eat the green microdots, people, or you'll be in for a *heavy* trip. If you have eaten one . . ."

I'd almost given up on Chris when I practically tripped over his body propped up against the base of the Monument.

"Hey, there, stranger," I greeted him. "You come here a lot?"

He gazed up at me blankly, a smile of recognition slowly spreading across his face. He was supremely wasted, and I noticed he had a small cut over his right brow.

"What happened there?" I motioned to the cut and slid down beside him on the pavement.

He touched his forehead, stared down at the caked blood on his hand, and shrugged. "Look at what I got—" He reached in his pocket and pulled out a handful of multicolored pills. "Here, you want some?" He held them out to me, spilling a few on the ground.

"What did you take, anyway?"

He sorted through his stash with his free hand. "One of these, and a couple of these . . . I think."

I took his hand and dumped its contents into my breast pocket. He seemed relieved to be rid of them and slumped back against the Monument. I leaned back too and gazed up the length of the huge stone slab, which seemed to vibrate with the amplified music.

Chris laughed softly beside me.

When I turned my head toward him, a single tear had paused on its way down the side of his face—a shiny glycerine droplet like you'd see on a movie star's cheek. I rested a hand on his shoulder. My head hurt, and suddenly it seemed like ages since we'd done something fun together, just for laughs. But if I sat perfectly still with my eyes and ears shut tight, I could almost pretend that we were back at Donnel School, just the two of us, sitting on a hillside on a warm autumn afternoon, when our biggest worry was getting caught by a master with our ties undone, and our grandest plans stretched all the way to dinnertime.

"It's time to go," he whispered hoarsely.

I was looking forward to the midnight fireworks, but he was in pretty bad shape. "Okay," I said. "You think you'll be able to ride your bike home?"

"No . . . man. Not home. It's time to *go*."

"Go where?"

"To Colorado." He started to get up, but I hauled him back down.

"We can't, man. The lab burned down with all our money. Remember?"

"Who needs money? We've got each other, right?"

"Right," I answered, hoping to humor him.

"So let's go."

"But . . . there'll be expenses."

"So we'll panhandle. We'll hitchhike. I bet there're a hundred people here from Colorado who'd give us a ride."

"Yeah, but . . . hey, let's talk about it tomorrow."

"No, man. Let's talk about it now." He was sobering up a little, which had me worried.

"What's to talk about?"

"Our trip. What's the matter? Don't you want to go?"

"Sure I do, but—"

"But what? Listen, if you don't want to go, just say so. It's a free country—nobody's making you."

But his eyes flashed dark and bright, pinning me to the wall.

"I want to go, Chris. It's just a matter of timing."

"Okay, so say a time. Tomorrow? Next week? When?"

Just then, as if on cue, the fireworks began. The sky exploded with light—pinwheels of light, starbursts of light. I closed my eyes, but the fireworks still made patterns inside my head.

When I opened my eyes, Chris was hovering over me, his face wild with light. I could feel him staring straight into my head, reading my mind.

"You don't want to go, do you? You never did. You were conning me all along, weren't you? And I bought it."

Then he began to laugh—a mad, mocking laugh—the way a coyote laughs at a full moon in the desert.

I shut my eyes and tried to sit totally still, still as stone against the Monument. But his voice slipped through again, quieter now. Sadder.

"Oh, man. Together we could've made it, you and me. We could have . . ."

The stone was cool against the back of my head. My shoulders were rigid now, my hips solid stone, like a statue. The music had stopped, and a voice came over the P.A. again, but I couldn't make out the words.

"So long, Danny-boy," someone whispered in my head.

When I opened my eyes he was gone. I tried to find him in the crowd, but I couldn't turn my head. I thought I saw him moving away through a group of dancing figures, but it was impossible to call his name. My throat had turned to solid rock.

Chapter Twenty-Four

I went back down to the monument grounds the next day and found his bike still locked to the tree where he'd left it. When his father called looking for him, I played dumb. I didn't hear from Chris the rest of the summer.

Then in early September Jimi Hendrix died. It was one of those pointless drug overdoses where the guy's partying hard one night, and the next morning they find him dead in a pool of vomit. Not too glamorous— and he was all of twenty-seven years old. I remember it happened on the first day of school, and suddenly all the rock stations were playing his songs and the deejays were making sad speeches and talking about him like he was dead or something, which of course he was, only it hadn't sunk in yet. I immediately thought of Chris, and wondered where he was and what he was doing when he heard the news.

I don't think the ski season had even started yet—it was just before Thanksgiving—when I heard Chris was back in town. My father told me he was at University Hospital, in the psychiatric ward.

I drove down there after school in my mother's old Dodge, the only car I was allowed to drive. I thought about stopping to pick up a present on the way, but that seemed like a dumb idea, so I bagged it.

When I signed in at the entrance to the psychiatric wing, I told them I was Chris's brother so they'd be sure to let me see him. Before I could get a pass, I had to empty all my pockets into a manila envelope, which they sealed and marked with my name: Daniel Jordan. Except for the locked door at the entrance, the psychiatric ward looked a lot like a college dorm, only cleaner. People walked around in normal clothing, and the rooms were furnished with bunk beds, dressers, and desks.

The door to Chris's room was ajar, and I could see him sitting on the lower bunk reading a ski magazine. I was surprised to find him looking the same. He was wearing jeans and a flannel shirt, and his hair was even longer than before. When I knocked on the door, I could tell he was surprised to see me, but I wasn't sure if he was pleased. He got up slowly from the bed and gave me a soul handshake, which I figured he'd picked up in Colorado.

"Relax," he said with a tight smile. "I haven't gone bonkers on you. I'm only here because my dad didn't want me thrown into the detox tank with the junkies and alkies. So they stuck me in here with the crazies. They may not look it, but they're all nuts up here. Yesterday my roommate tried to throw a chair through the window and jump out after it. So now he's in isolation and I've got a single." He laughed briefly to himself. "Personally, I'd rather be tagged a junkie than a schizo, but they say the food's better up here."

We were standing face to face, but somehow our eyes wouldn't meet.

"So siddown, make yourself comfortable. And don't mind my jabbering. The drugs they give me make me talk a blue streak. Isn't that wild? They try to cure a druggie with drugs." He laughed aloud and pulled me down onto the bed. There was definitely something different about his laugh.

"So," I said, looking for an opening, "what do you do here all day?"

"Mostly lie around and wait for the nurse to bring my medicine. Then they send me down to Occupational Therapy. They're very big on O.T. here, only I don't find it so therapeutic. First day on the ward they ask me what kind of O.T. I want. Basically there's woodworking and basket weaving. No kidding, they really have basket weaving. So naturally I pick woodwork. Only since this is a nuthouse, they can't let you use real tools. So their idea of woodwork turns out to be making models with balsa wood and Elmer's glue. Now *that'll* make you crazy. You ever try to work with *balsa* wood? You can't do shit with balsa."

He stopped talking, finally out of breath. I guessed it was my turn again. "I, uh, I'm sorry Colorado didn't work out."

He shrugged and cracked his knuckles hard. "So what about you? You got wheels yet?"

"Not my own. But I got a license and I can usually use my mom's car."

"That's good. I wonder if I can get a license, being a junkie who's done time in a loony bin and all.

I shrugged. "I don't see why not."

"Sure, why not? Hey—it's feeding time!"

A nurse rolled a small cart into the room. Not a TV-style nurse, exactly, but not bad-looking. If she hadn't worn so much makeup, she would've been cute.

"This lady just can't get enough of my ass."

"That's right," she said with a smirk, "so whip it out."

"You want me to . . . uh, wait in the hall?" I asked.

"No, don't go. Who knows, if you play your cards right, old Marge here might fix you up too."

Chris pulled his pants down halfway and swung his rear around toward the nurse. She filled a hypo from a small glass vial, then dabbed one of his cheeks with alcohol and slid the needle in.

When she was done, Chris slipped down into bed, lolling over on his back. "The earth really moved for me, Marge. Was it good for you?"

"Swell," she snorted. "You know, you're not supposed to be enjoying this. That's how you got into trouble in the first place." She wheeled the cart out of the room.

"See you tonight, sweetheart," Chris called after her.

He giggled softly to himself and watched her disappear down the hall. But when he turned back to me, he wasn't smiling anymore. His eyes were glazed over, but somehow piercing all the same.

"So what gives?" he asked coldly. "What are you doing here?"

"What do you think? I wanted to see you."

"Well who asked you? Did I?"

"I just heard you were back in town, so naturally I wanted to see you."

"Just heard I was back in town, huh? Just wanted to see me? Well, how do I look?" I didn't say anything. "What do you want from me?"

"Well . . . now that you're back, I thought . . . I was hoping we could be friends again."

"Is that right? Now that I'm back from my little

Rocky Mountain vacation, we can just pick up where we left off. After all, nothing's changed."

"I didn't say nothing's changed. I just said I wanted to be friends."

"That's a sweet thought, Danny-boy. But I'm not in the market for a friend right now." He looked straight through me. "We tried that one already, and it didn't work out so hot, remember?"

He pulled himself up from the bed. "Now, if you'll excuse me, I'm due downstairs at O.T. There's a model of the *Santa Maria* that requires my immediate attention."

So he walked out of the room without looking back, and left me sitting there on the lower bunk. After a few minutes I went down to my car. I started the motor, but I couldn't seem to move out of the underground garage. I felt as if someone was watching me from inside my rearview mirror. When I finally checked, I met my own accusing eyes staring back at me. They knew I was relieved that it was over, that he wouldn't let me back into his life now that things had gone bad.

The link was severed. Chris disengaged like a spent rocket booster and fell dead away toward earth. So now I was free to continue my solo ascent toward the heavens and a liberal arts education.

I never saw Chris again. And what I heard about him from other people sounded bad—a couple of car wrecks, a couple of busts. So when that late night call came from my father, it didn't exactly take me by surprise. I'd already imagined it in my mind a dozen times, a dozen different ways.

Chapter Twenty-Five

They unhooked the machines the day after I got back to Washington.

I didn't cry at the funeral. I don't know why. Maybe because there were so many people there. When my great-grandfather died, almost all his friends were dead already, so there wasn't much of a turnout at his funeral. Chris didn't have that problem. The church was so packed, you'd have thought it was Easter Sunday. I knew some of the kids by sight, but I did a lot of double takes. Guys I'd only seen in jeans and T-shirts were standing around in suits tugging at their neckties. I probably looked just as strange.

I could see Chris's parents collapsed into seats in the front pew. Lots of people were going up to talk to them in low voices, but I didn't have anything to say. The only person I wanted to see was Debbie. When I touched her arm, she turned around real quick and startled. She opened her mouth as if to say something—but nothing came out. Then her head kind of fell forward onto my shoulder and we hugged each other while she cried. It made me feel old, but in a bad way. I'd always wanted to hold her, always wondered what it would feel like.

It felt lousy—and no matter how tight I held her, she wouldn't stop crying.

When the funeral finally started, I stood alone in the back of the church while the minister made some speech about how there was nothing to say at times like this. But then he went on to talk about how we should all circle round and comfort each other. I didn't want to circle round with this crowd, especially not the adults. All those overdressed mothers whispering to each other— "What a tragedy. Such a handsome boy, too"—when mostly they were just relieved it wasn't their kid who fucked up so bad.

There wasn't much religious stuff in the service. I think the Jordans were Unitarians, which means they believe in God, only he's really a person, or something like that. At the end of the ceremony they played a recording of George Harrison's "My Sweet Lord" just to show how hip and groovy they were, but the volume was turned way down and the speakers were shot anyway. It's weird, but I kept expecting Chris to pop up out of the casket, laughing his head off at the great joke he'd pulled on everyone.

By the time we got to the cemetery, they already had the hole dug out, and I knew it wasn't a joke. There were these two uniformed guys standing around waiting to bury him, but they weren't folksy old gravediggers like in *Hamlet*. They looked more like union guys putting in their eight hours. They lowered him down on a motorized pulley, then stood aside and had a smoke while the minister recited a prayer and threw a handful of dirt into the grave. That was pretty much it, and since it was cold as a bitch, everyone cleared out fast.

I decided to stick around and watch the Teamsters finish their job. They went at it like a couple of construction workers. One of them plowed the dirt back into the hole with a minitractor while the other guy packed it down with a flatheaded jackhammer. Then they rolled out a fresh piece of sod, pounded it down good, and stuck a small plastic marker on top:

CHRISTOPHER JORDAN 1955–1974.

After the funeral everyone went back to the Jordans' house to eat and drink and pretend it was a party or something. I didn't want to go, but my mom said I should, for Kitty's sake. So I hung out in the kitchen, drinking scotch and watching the caterers unwrap food and glasses. Nellie wasn't working that day. She was dressed in her best black outfit like all the other mourners. But still, she couldn't keep from poking her head into the kitchen every few minutes to see what the caterers were up to.

When she spotted me leaning against the back door, she came over and gave me a hug. Up close, I could tell she'd been crying.

"You were a good friend to him," she said.

I just shrugged.

"That's why I'm askin' you to do this."

"Do what?"

She looked around to see if any of the caterers were listening, but they were busy fussing over a smoked turkey. "I want you to clean out his room," she said in a hushed voice.

"What do you mean?"

"I know Mrs. Jordan's gonna go through his things, and I don't want her finding anything she shouldn't. It would just break her heart."

I nodded my head slowly and weaved out into the hallway. I guess I was a little drunk by then, and it took me a while to make it through the crowd and up the stairs to his room.

I shut the door and leaned my back against it. Very little had changed since the last time I was there. The Hendrix posters from the clubhouse were still hanging on the wall. The black light was there too.

It didn't take me long to find Chris's stash. There was a goddamn pharmacy crammed into the back of his speaker cabinets—vials of pills, tiny bags of powder, and a fat lump of hash. I carried it all into the bathroom and flushed it down the toilet.

As I was watching all that garbage swirl down the bowl, something flashed in my head. Gently I raised the top of the toilet tank, and sure enough, his works were there, taped up under the lid—a length of rubber hose, a syringe, and two sterile needles still sealed in plastic.

I didn't know what to do with the stuff, so I just crammed it into my jacket pocket. Then I locked the bathroom door and sat down on the toilet seat. I'd finally found a safe place to cry.

When I was done, I went back to his room and lay

down on the bed. I switched on the black light, and the Hendrix posters sprang to life, glowering like two masks on the wall. I couldn't resist fishing through the record pile till I found a Hendrix album to put on the turntable. Hell—no one can cry like Jimi's guitar.

> *Drifting*
> *on a sea of forgotten tear drops,*
> *on a lifeboat,*
> *sailing home . . .*

I fell asleep there on Chris's bed. When Nellie woke me, the party was over and everyone else had gone home.

Chapter Twenty-Six

I went back to school and flunked my Chaucer exam. That's the one thing I learned—even when your best friend dies the rest of the world keeps right on going without a blink, especially the world of exams. I'd never flunked a test before, but it wasn't nearly as bad as I'd always imagined. There're a lot of worse things.

You might say I got sort of morbidly obsessed for a while. I found myself taking philosophy and religion courses the next semester, just to see what some of the heavy hitters had to say on the subject of the big D. I didn't come away with much, though. Those guys are all in love with capitalized words like Faith and Will and Fate. Fate didn't mean much to me anymore. It was just a word.

All spring, I kept having these dreams about Chris. They weren't really nightmares, but they were scary all the same, because he seemed so alive in them. He'd talk and joke, as real as day. Sometimes in the dream I'd remember he was dead, but most of the time I didn't. Until I woke up, and then I'd realize it was just a dream, and Chris was probably worm feed by now. It made me kind of crazy.

Blairsville High School Library

It got so I wasn't sleeping much, even after school ended and I was back home for the summer. One morning I was up early and having breakfast with my father, who was on his way to the hospital to operate. I asked him if he was scared the first time he ever cut into someone, back in medical school or whenever. He said yeah, sure he was. Then I asked him how long it was before he stopped being scared. He didn't say anything for a while. Then he looked up from the newspaper and shot me this nervous half smile, which I knew meant it never really stopped being scary. He could have fooled me with some line about being a pro or something, but instead he gave me that look, like a gift, so I'd know that about him.

I'm still finding out stuff about Chris. I figure those dreams are the part of him that got inside me, that's mine for keeps. That's all you ever really have of someone else—the part they give you and let you hold inside.

So you might as well let go of the rest.